NORMAL LIKE US is anything but. One of the many finely drawn characters in this collection begins to suspect that happiness lurks "in the small moments when no one seems to be noticing." Except Peterson does, and can make you mourn and cherish those moments as few other writers can. Open these stories carefully; they'll catch you like a Venus flytrap.

—Paul Willis, professor of English, Westmont College
and author of
BRIGHT SHOOTS OF EVERLASTINGNESS:
Essays on Faith and the American Wild

These stories take us down trails that we have been down many times before. We thought we knew them as well as the back of our hand. We don't. Peterson's stories open our eyes and ears to miracles in the ordinary. You will walk with a lighter step. The mountains skip like rams, the hills like lambs. You will too when you read these stories.

—Eugene H. Peterson
author of RUN WITH THE HORSES

Normal
Like Us

ALSO BY LEIF PETERSON

Catherine Wheels
a novel

Normal Like Us

Stories

LEIF PETERSON

StylusInk

NORMAL LIKE US
Copyright © 2008 by Leif Peterson
ALL RIGHTS RESERVED

Printed in the United States of America
2008—First Edition

10 9 8 7 6 5 4 3 2 1

Special thanks to the following publications in which many of these stories originally appeared:

Porcupine Literary Arts Magazine: "Kidneys & Bullet Holes"
Pindeldyboz: "Satisfaction Guaranteed"
Word Riot: "Phase Twelve"
Montana Quarterly: "It's Darkest in Suburbia,"
"A Girl & A Chainsaw," and "Walking on Water"
Rosebud: "The Inept"
Ruminate: "Angels Don't Sleep"
Whitefish Review: "Fordicidia"

Peterson, Leif 1965—
Normal Like Us; stories / by Leif Peterson
p. cm.
1. Stories—Fiction. I. Title.

ISBN 9781-4196-8494-9 (paper)

So many stories…

this is for Amy

contents

KIDNEYS & BULLET HOLES

THIS IS NEW. The woman next to me is on dialysis. In the room I was in before there was just an old man who breathed through a hole in his throat. He had to cover up the hole with his finger to talk. I thought that had potential at first, but then I realized he was just an old man who happened to have a hole in his throat. You'd think someone with that kind of life experience would have volumes of interesting things to say, but I could tell after five minutes that life had depleted him, not filled him up. After that there was nothing.

This room is larger and more comfortable. It's in a quieter part of the hospital. I'm out of danger now and they don't think they have to check in on me all the time. That's fine with me. I'm happy to be left alone, especially now that I have the woman on dialysis to talk to. Her name is Katie. She's only twenty-four. She's asleep now, but a little while ago, when they first moved me, she was awake, and we talked. I don't think I'll get bored with her for a long time. We're going to have fun together because she thinks the way I do. Hey, two bullet holes in your back or a worthless set of kidneys. Who cares. We're going to have a good time. This is our attitude about life. It's the way we think. I didn't always think this way. I think when the balcony collapsed it was a turning point, or the weeks after.

I seem to have this propensity for meeting my lovers in hospital rooms. I remember glancing across a crowded room where smoke hung like cirrus near the ceiling and seeing Maggie, but it wasn't until the next day in the hospital room that we met. She was sitting by my bed when I woke up. She had little furrows at the corners of her eyes like a plowed field.

"Do you remember me?" she asked.

I told her that I did, because she seemed vaguely familiar and I didn't want to hurt her feelings, but it wasn't until later that I was able to remember anything about the party.

"I was at the party," she said just to make sure.

"And we danced," I said.

"No. But I wanted you to ask me."

She came again the next day and by then I'd remembered more about the party. She sat by my bed and crossed her legs and handed me the newspaper.

"Have you seen this?"

I took the paper and looked at it. The front page was completely dedicated to the balcony collapse at the party. There was a picture of the superintendent of the building standing in front of the wreckage. There was a mustard-yellow bulldozer in the corner of the picture. The superintendent was quoted as saying that it was a terrible tragedy, but that the balcony had never been designed for that many people. I looked at Maggie.

"Four people died," I said. "I didn't know that."

"It was terrible," said Maggie.

I considered my reflection in the television screen hanging from the ceiling in the corner. My legs and back ached, like I'd spent the entire night shoveling gravel.

"Do you remember the paramedics?" asked Maggie.

"I don't think so."

"Do you know what a compound fracture is?" she asked.

"I think so."

"It's when a broken bone breaks through your skin. That's what happened to your leg."

I looked at her face. Her skin was brown and smooth, and the wrinkles at the corners of her eyes had a familiarity that I couldn't place. She was wearing a blouse the color of delphiniums, unbuttoned at the neck, exposing some of the skin between her breasts. I thought she had a little bit of an accent, not something foreign, but something regional.

"When the paramedics pulled you away from the wreckage and had you on a stretcher, you looked down and saw the bone sticking out of your thigh."

"I don't remember."

"I think you were in shock, but you were actually quite lucid. You said something funny."

"What did I say?"

"You said, I bet that's going to hurt in the morning."

"What did the paramedic say?"

"She asked how much you'd had to drink."

I remembered a finger held up in front of my face, and a tiny flashlight. The woman's voice coming from somewhere else, maybe from beneath the earth. *That's right. Watch my finger. Can you tell me your name?*

I've been trying to figure out a way to get a look at my back. I think when Katie wakes up I'll roll over on my side and ask her to describe what she sees. She seems like someone who could do a pretty good job describing something. Some people look at something like that and all they can do is have some kind of emotional reaction. That's no good. I have a friend who's a writer. He could look into a barrel of lopped-off heads and describe it so beautifully you'd think it was nothing but a jar of pickles. That's talent.

Katie has talent. I first noticed it when I told her how I got these bullet holes in my back. When I told the old man with the hole in his throat, his eyes widened and he started making these gurgling sounds with his ruined throat that were supposed to show his concern. When I told Katie, she just laughed. She laughed so hard I thought she was going to pop a gasket on that machine she's attached to. It seems to me that's the right reaction. I mean, it was funny. I mean, what could be funnier? I can already hear what Katie will say when she looks at my back. She'll use a word like *august*. She'll compare it to the pockmarked buildings at Pearl Harbor. She'll use the language of a steelworker. It's refreshing to know someone like her, to know there are still people like her in the world, people that haven't been crushed.

Maggie didn't come the next day, but she came the day after. She was wearing the delphinium blouse again, which made me wonder if I hadn't lost a day or two somewhere. She sat down next to the bed and touched my arm.

"How are you feeling?"

"Pretty good. A nurse was just here with some painkillers."

"Do you want to get out of here? I got permission from your doctor. I thought we could have a little picnic."

A wheelchair arrived and she rolled me out to her car. I had to sit in the back seat because my leg wouldn't bend, but once I was in it wasn't that uncomfortable. There was a canvas bag on the floor. I spied a baguette and a bottle of wine and a silver thermos. It was a sunny day and it was good to be away from the astringent smell of the hospital. Maggie put on dark sunglasses and drove us to a park along the river. While she wrestled the wheelchair out of the trunk I looked out over the rolling lawns and saw a man throwing a Frisbee for his dog. The dog would leap four or five feet off the ground to catch the Frisbee then bring it back like it was a pheasant or a grouse. I looked down at my leg and remembered the slow shifting of the balcony. There was the wrenching sound of metal and a sudden hush as everyone stopped talking. Even as it was happening I was looking around at people's faces, reading their thoughts. But no one looked like they had a millstone around their neck. It was just the opposite. Like we were about to fly.

I've told some of the nurses about how I'm an FBI agent and I'm always breaking up drug deals. Sometimes I take a few slugs, I say. This always gets them. Sometimes I see the younger nurses point at me from the hall and giggle. They know they shouldn't believe a word I say, but they still regard me as some kind of hero. They've somehow gotten the impression that I had some role in breaking up the robbery. I let them believe what they will. I don't feel like telling the truth anymore. It depresses me when the beautiful absurdity of a story is lost just because it happens to be true.

But nothing is lost on Katie, so when she wakes up and asks me about my life, I'll just give it to her straight. I'll tell her about Maggie. About how things turned out. And she'll understand. She'll understand where I've been and the journey I've taken. She has a nose for the wonderful absurdity of life. She has a sardonic wit that I find compelling. I can just hear Katie saying, There's time for a mournful demeanor, but today is not that day.

Maggie laid out a blanket on the grass and helped me out of the chair. There were ducks circling near the shore hoping for some of the baguette. I leaned on one elbow and looked at Maggie unpacking the canvas bag. There was a warm feeling between us, something understood. The afternoon light glistened in her Navajo-brown hair. I noticed the veins on the back of her hands, like inverted canals on the surface of Mars.

"Do you want a glass of wine?" asked Maggie.

"Just a little," I said. "The painkillers."

We spread soft cheese on the baguette and ate grapes from a plastic bowl. Maggie sliced pieces of peppered salami that made the sides of my nose sweat. The ducks came up on the shore and stood near us waiting. There were low willows on the bank of the river that were just beginning to leaf out. The wine was dry and leathery and smelled of pipe smoke. It made me feel warm all over.

Maggie looked at me and smiled with her eyes. Then there was a long moment when we just stared at each other.

"I was on the balcony," she said at last.

I didn't say anything. The cocktail of painkillers and wine and sunshine made me want to close my eyes and sleep.

"Just five or ten minutes before it collapsed. I was out

10 / Leif Peterson

there getting some air."

She reached out and pushed the hair away from my eyes.

"I saw you go down," she said. "I was watching you because you reminded me of someone. I was hoping you were going to come in and ask me to dance."

Sometimes people misinterpret a shared traumatic event as fate. But mostly they're just random events that we like to attach significance to.

I reached over and touched one of the veins on the back of Maggie's hand.

"Why are you sad?" I asked, but even as I was saying it I was closing my eyes.

The great thing about Katie is that she knows how to have fun. You can be sardonic without being cynical. I bet if the machine she's attached to ever spit out a cloud of blue smoke and ground to a halt, she'd just look at me and make a joke. How'd you do in auto shop? she'd say. Or, You wouldn't happen to have a Phillips-head screwdriver on you, would ya? That's Katie for you, always ready with a joke. I watch her while she sleeps. Even in sleep she seems assured that life can't dole out more mist and fog than she's capable of seeing through. When she's through with her dialysis I'll take her on a picnic like the ones Maggie and I used to go on. Maybe we'll have to haul the dialysis machine along with us, but that will just enrich the experience. Sometimes adversity is what reminds us that we're alive. Have a near death experience one day, quit your job the next. Isn't that the way it usually works? If not, it should be. Maybe I'll suggest to Katie a trip to the zoo. Maybe I'll suggest we set something free.

When I woke up the sun was just skimming the scalloped tops of the faraway woods. Maggie was down at the water's edge, throwing the remnants of our bread to the ducks. My leg and back were beginning to throb. I fixed my eyes on her narrow shoulders and tried to remember. Had she told me that her brother had recently died, or was that part of a dream? Had there been an explosion?

Maggie looked at me over her shoulder. She tossed away the rest of the bread and came and sat down.

"It's cooling off," she said. "Do you want to go?"

"Okay."

I started putting things away in the canvas bag, but Maggie leaned over and kissed me. When she pulled away there was a bright jet trail over her head. I touched the fine lapel of her delphinium blouse and watched her lips part then press back together. She kissed me again and smiled.

"I have been," she said. "But not anymore."

I stared at her vacantly.

"Sad," she said. "I have been. But not anymore."

Katie and I both believe in the randomness of life. If you're the least bit observant it's hard to come away with a much different conclusion. But I guess we would both allow that it could also be more than that. We're not willing to say it isn't. The real trick, at least for Katie and me, is to keep things in perspective. There are, after all, two ways to look at everything. If your car breaks down you could, on one hand, think what a miserable life you have. Or, you could realize that it could have been much worse, that the car that picked you up might not have come along for hours, that it could have been something much worse than a burned-up bearing, that it could have been raining. You're lucky really. Just think of all the people in the world that are worse off. Katie and I have been in the hospital a time or two. But hey, we're on the third floor, aren't we? Our room has windows. We're not down in the basement where the rooms are refrigerated and all the patients have toe tags.

It must have been the weekend, because Maggie showed up in the middle of the day to help me go home. My mother had offered to fly in for a few days and help out, but I told her I'd be fine.

"I'm not an invalid," I said. "It's just a broken leg."

My mother was the kind of person who could un-hem a pair of jeans so they'd slip over a cast, the kind of woman who wouldn't mind doing her son's laundry for a week. But she was also the kind of woman prone to rearranging kitchen utensils, the kind of woman who would silently disapprove of the dead flies in the overhead light fixtures, the kind of woman who would say, *I just can't abide a dirty kitchen...but yours is fine.* She's also like a Venus flytrap with strangers. Any chance encounter can turn into a lifelong relationship. I once heard her talk forty-five minutes on the phone to a wrong number. Her Christmas card mailing list runs into the thousands.

But there was none of that when Maggie walked into the apartment. She just helped me to the couch and asked if she could get me anything. When I told her I was fine she looked around for a moment then stared down at her hands.

"Well," she said. "I guess I'll bring up the groceries."

When she started putting the groceries away I told her she didn't need to, but she said she was happy to do it. Afterward she made us a little dinner, which we ate on the couch while we watched TV. She kissed me a couple times, which felt nice, but the painkillers were making me so relaxed I didn't have much energy for kissing back.

"It's okay," said Maggie. "I'll help you to bed."

The funny thing is I wasn't really tired, just incredibly relaxed. I lay in bed for a long time after she left and watched the lights from passing cars flash across the ceiling and down the wall. I heard the neighbors upstairs arguing. Their voices rose and fell in pitch like rolling waves. After a while they quieted down. I imagined they'd moved to the bedroom to make everything better. In the morning I woke up with my leg throbbing and looked around for where Maggie had left my pills. I found them on the bathroom vanity where I also found her watch. I wondered if she'd just forgotten it or if this was the kind of thing women do on purpose.

Katie's not the type to play games. She believes a

relationship should be based on honesty. When she wakes up, if she doesn't feel like talking, she'll just say so. She's not the kind to say someone "passed on" or is "using the powder room." For her, euphemisms are a form of dishonesty, like watering down the truth. When she wakes up I'll ask her if she knows anyone who's gone down to the slumber room and she'll throw whatever she has at hand in my direction.

"It's a *morgue*," she'll say. "Say it. *Morgue.*"

But she'll know I'm kidding.

The day I got the cast off Maggie took me out to dinner to celebrate. She met me at the doctor's office just as we were finishing up.

"How's it look?" she asked.

"Skinny," I said.

"Does he need to be careful?" she asked the doctor. "What can he do?"

"Jog. Run. Jump. Play basketball," said the doctor. "Once he regains his muscle, it'll be stronger than it used to be."

We went to a sushi bar downtown. Maggie thought the protein would be good for me. Afterward we drove out to the beach and took a walk. There was a crescent moon rising out of the ocean and the sand sparkled in the moonlight. We took off our shoes and held hands. The night was warm and Maggie's skin smelled of melons. There was a feeling inside me that I couldn't name, except that it was new. I stopped walking and held both of Maggie's hands.

"For the last six weeks you've been taking care of me," I said. "Now I'd like to take care of you."

Maggie looked at me and smiled then looked out to the ocean, the moonlight reflecting in her eyes.

"It doesn't work that way," she said. "I took care of you because it was necessary and because I wanted to. It's not something to pay back."

"That's not what I meant."

"Didn't you?"

There was a long moment of silence, just the crashing of the waves.

"You told me once I reminded you of someone," I said. "Who was it? A lover that died?"

"No," she said. "My brother."

We walked on until we saw a dark spot in the sand. When we got close we saw that it was a seal that had been beheaded. We stopped and looked. I was aware that it was a testing moment, that Maggie's reaction could be a moment in time divided into before and after.

Her hand dropped from mine and she hugged herself across the chest.

"Let's go," she said. "I'm getting cold."

In that moment I knew the sadness would never leave her, that it would always be the fulcrum on which all her other emotions were balanced. At the same time I knew it was wrong of me to expect anything else. Years later I would think of that walk again and imagine how different it would have been if it had been Katie with me. She would have taken my hand, given a little squeeze, a squeeze full of empathy; then she would have suggested vegetarian burritos and carrot juice at the nearby taquería. At a moment like that, I would not have been able to contain my love for her.

Back at the car we sat for a while before leaving. Maggie had both hands on the wheel, but she made no move to turn the ignition.

"Let's do something," she said.

"Okay."

She looked at me through the shark-gray light that filled the car. Her eyes were filled with the memory of her brother.

"Let's go to the zoo and set something free."

Getting into the zoo only required climbing a twelve-foot stone wall and navigating the wrought-iron spikes on top, but once in we found ourselves at a loss as to how to set anything free. All the cages and buildings were locked. Even if we could have unlocked a cage, at that hour I don't think the animals would have been inclined to leave.

I suggested we go home, but Maggie wasn't ready to give up. We walked around for a while, checking doors and windows and cages, but it was really futile. When I suggested again that we just go home Maggie started to cry. She slumped down on the cement with her legs crossed and sobbed into her hands.

I knelt next to her and put my arm around her.

"It's okay," I said. "We'll find something. I didn't mean that about going home."

"You don't understand," said Maggie, still sobbing.

"Today is my brother's birthday."

I know Katie and I don't have much future. She knows it too. The transplant list is a mile long. But there's no sense getting bitter. Life is full of surprises. It'll crack you up if you're just on the lookout for it. Look at me. I'm staggering up the street with a queen-sized mattress on my back when two hooded teenagers come running out of a liquor store and the owner fires two bullets through the mattress and into my back. The first thing the doctor says to me when I wake up is, You're very lucky to be alive. That mattress saved your life. He really said that. And he meant it. He was serious. He didn't even think it was funny. I mean, would you want to go through life missing things like that?

IT'S DARKEST IN SUBURBIA

IT'S THE SUMMER after my senior year of college, that summer when the embassy in Kenya is bombed, when the neighbor across the street cuts off his fingers, the summer I take up smoking.

I'm home for the summer, home for three last months of sweltering Maryland heat before making a clean break and moving on to the next thing. I know there's no such thing as a truly clean break. There are always tendrils that stretch but don't break, but I'm doing what comes as close to a truly clean break as anything I can imagine.

The smoking, although temporary, is out of character—no one in our family has ever smoked, except for my aunt who died from it—but my parents are surprisingly nonjudgmental. The first time I light up in front of them my mother gives a little gasp and puts her hand to her throat as if she is having trouble breathing. Maybe she's remembering her sister, how she slowly shriveled up and finally died when she weighed less than ninety pounds. But all she says is, "Oh, honey, you're not doing that, are you?"

My father waits a couple days before saying anything and when he does it is only to ask me to keep it on the back porch. He doesn't have to say, "So the neighbors won't see." He's the Presbyterian minister in town and as much as he hates it, he has to keep up appearances. He drives all the way down to Baltimore County to buy his beer. He, more than anyone else, can probably understand the smoking. He can probably intuit, without me having to say anything, that it's temporary, a phase, and yet necessary.

The back porch is fine with me. I'm not trying to make a statement. I'm not being rebellious. I've simply done some growing up in college. I've grown out of my sheltered suburban naiveté. There's just something I can't name inside me, and smoking seems to fit with it.

Besides the smoking being temporary, what I haven't told my parents yet, what I haven't even told Carly, is that at the end of the summer I'm going out West. I've arranged for a job on a fifteen-thousand-acre sheep ranch just outside of Three Forks, Montana. They supply the horse, the food, the bullets. All I have to show up with is a rifle and a decent pair of boots. Then it will just be me and the sheep and an endless sea of sagebrush. Sometimes I close my eyes and think about it, and when I do, I can smell the sagebrush. That pungency fills my lungs and doesn't leave room for anything else. I already have the appropriate symbolic moment planned for the bus station. When the bus pulls in I'm going to light up a cigarette and throw whatever's left of the pack into the nearest trash can. When the cigarette is done I'm going to exhale the last of the smoke and everything else with it and climb on. From then on out it will just be sheep, sagebrush and horizon.

Carly always calls late in the morning, and usually I'm still in bed. My mother knocks gently on the door and when I don't answer she sticks her head in and says, "Scott, dear, the phone's for you. It's Carly. What should I tell her? Were you planning to get up today?"

I take the phone to the back porch and light up the day's first cigarette.

"What's wrong?" asks Carly.

"Nothing," I say. "Why do you ask?"

"Because something is. What is it?"

"Nothing," I say. "I'm bored. It's hot."

"You said you wanted to be bored. You said that's why you wanted to go home for the summer."

"I know. I do. I didn't say I was unhappy about it. I'm perfectly happy being bored."

"Then what's wrong?"

"Nothing's wrong," I say. "Why do you insist there's something wrong?" There's an edginess creeping into my voice and I take a deep drag on the cigarette to try to squelch it.

"If you're so unhappy maybe you should just come to Iowa and help me look for an apartment."

"I really think I want to stay here for the summer," I say. "I trust you to find an apartment."

Carly and I both applied to the graduate school at Iowa and I had to muster a good bit of false disappointment when she was accepted and I was not. It wasn't something I was sure I wanted to do. As was the case with most things in our relationship, I was simply being carried along in the wake of her plans, her enthusiasm. But Carly wouldn't give up. She proposed that we both move to Ames and I could work while she went to school. Meanwhile I would reapply for the spring term.

"It's easier to get in in the spring," said Carly. "There's always some new openings."

This is something that I would say we have discussed and considered, but Carly would say that we have already decided.

I don't know why I can't tell her about the sheep ranch.

She's already in Ames.

"What's the temperature there?" I ask.

I hope she doesn't notice the non sequitur.

There's a long silence, then Carly's voice again, sounding tired.

"Okay, Scott," she says. "Let's talk about the weather."

"No, I'm serious," I say. "I want to know."

"Seventy-seven," says Carly. "On the way to a high of eighty-four. Chance of local afternoon thunderstorms. Overnight low expected to be in the high sixties. How about there?"

She's being mockingly cheerful, but I don't let it get to me.

"Already up to ninety," I say. "And the humidity is like a thousand percent."

There's another long silence. Somewhere in the distance a lawn mower starts up. Inside the house my mother is in the kitchen, washing the breakfast dishes and listening to NPR.

"Why don't you come to Iowa?" asks Carly. "I miss you."

In the distance the lawn mower chugs to a halt, then in a moment restarts.

"I miss you too," I say to Carly. "I'll think about it."

In the kitchen my mother is standing at the sink in an apron scrubbing willfully at a nonstick skillet.

"What's for breakfast?" I say.

She doesn't even turn around.

"Up at the crack of eleven-thirty, I see. Breakfast was at eight."

When did everyone get so serious?

I walk up behind her and put my hands on her shoulders. It occurs to me that she may be shrinking. I bend down and kiss her on the cheek.

"I'm kidding," I say. "I'll just have a cup of coffee to take the chill off."

"The heat is not my fault, Scott," she says.

I pour myself a cup of coffee and sit down at the kitchen table.

"I didn't say it was," I say. "Is something wrong?"

She waits a minute. I can see her tiny shoulders tensing as she scours at the skillet.

"I don't know how anyone with a conscience could call this nonstick," she says.

"They don't last forever," I say. "You're probably due for a new one."

"I suppose they taught you all about Teflon at college?"

I look out the window where a squirrel is attempting to leap from a tree branch into the bird feeder. He maneuvers his way as far out on a shaky limb as he can, then suddenly he leaps and misses. On the ground he examines his paws for a moment as if it might be their fault that he's missed, then he's up the tree again for another try. I look back to my mother at the sink. There seems to be a tangible wall of humidity between us.

"Is there a pawn shop in town?" I ask.

"Why?" asks my mother. "Are you planning to hock my silver?"

"No, I'm planning to buy a rifle."

She turns around and dries her hands on a towel.

"Good Lord, Scott. When did this happen? When did we stop being friends? Do you remember what good friends we used to be?

I look at her, then down at my coffee.

"We're still friends," I say. "I really am going to buy a rifle."

She goes back to her skillet, scrubbing with the entirety of her upper body, then suddenly she stops and walks over to the trash can and drops the skillet in. Without looking at me she removes her apron, hangs it on the back of the pantry door and walks out of the kitchen.

"There are no pawn shops," she says as she leaves. "This is a respectable town. You'll have to go into the city to get your rifle."

On the back porch that evening I sit and smoke and stare at the thermometer, which refuses to dip below ninety even though the sun is down. When my father appears I crush out the half-smoked cigarette and give him a nod. He's holding two sweaty bottles of beer. He hands me one as he sits. He takes a few sips before he talks.

"How'd you manage to pass your day," he asks.

"I went into the city and bought a gun," I say. "How about you?"

My father smiles briefly, then looks into his beer and takes another sip.

"Two funerals," he says. "Back to back."

"People from your congregation?" I ask.

"I'm afraid not," he says. "I hardly knew them. Barely knew their families."

"That must be hard," I say. "Burying someone you don't know. Knowing what to say."

"It's no picnic," he says.

"How do you do it?"

My father looks across the lawn, but his eyes seem unfocused. From several houses away comes the sound of AM radio.

"I try to talk less about the person who has died and more about what God wants from us," he says. "I try to emphasize that we're not long for this earth so we should be striving for excellence."

I look to the back of the lawn where a neighbor's cat is stalking a robin. My father gets up and returns with two fresh beers.

"Do you like living here?" I ask.

"What do you mean? You mean in suburbia?"

"Yeah."

My father laughs. A quick laugh that seems cut short. He looks at me and smiles and I notice for the first time the crow's feet around his eyes.

"I can't stand it," he says.

"Then why don't you leave?" I ask.

He looks up to the sky as if he's expecting a storm to move in.

"I guess I feel I have a ministry here," he says. "To show people that God wants more from them than they want for themselves. To wake them up a little. To show them that there's more to life than swimming pools and boats and owning a condo at the shore and buying a new car every two years."

"Do you ever succeed?" I ask.

My father drinks from his beer and looks out sadly over the lawn.

"I don't know, Scott," he says. "I don't know if I ever do."

I've bought a pair of cowboy boots and a hat and I wear them all the time despite the heat. I walk out into the yard and rub dirt into the boots. I purposefully scuff them against each other when I walk. I don't want them looking new when I show up at the ranch. The hat already has a nice circle of sweat around the rim and I've begun to reshape it a little in the front so it will hang down over my eyes.

Carly calls to tell me she's found an apartment. It's in the basement of a house and a little damp, but big.

"It's also a little more than I was hoping to spend," she says, "but with you working and my assistantship, we'll be fine."

"Carly," I say, "I don't have a job yet."

"I've been working on that," she says. "I already have a couple of possibilities."

"Like what?" I ask.

"Well, for one," says Carly, "one of the professor's wives owns a florist shop in town. I met her the other day and she said she was looking for a new delivery person."

"You want me to deliver flowers?" I ask.

"I don't know," she says. "It's just one of the first things I've come across. It might be fun. I'll keep looking. It would be a lot easier if you were out here. Is there any possibility of that?"

"Anything's possible," I say. "I'll think about it."

I sit on the back porch and smoke and listen to the radio. It's already August and I can't think of one thing I've done all summer. The telephone rings and I hear my mother answer. The telephone rings twelve or fifteen times a day and sometimes the calls can last for up to an hour. I don't know how my mother ever gets anything done.

The music on the radio stops and the news comes on. I learn that the U.S. Embassy in Kenya has been bombed by terrorists. The phone rings again and this time it's Carly. It's not usual for her to call in the middle of the day, but then I remember: Her college roommate is in Kenya for the summer. I try to remember what she's doing there, if she's working at the embassy.

When I hang up the phone my mother is chopping onions on the counter. She turns to me with tears in her eyes.

"Everything all right?" she asks.

I push the cowboy hat back a little on my head.

"The U.S. Embassy in Kenya was bombed," I say. "Carly's roommate was there, but she's okay."

"Good Lord," she says. "Good gracious Lord."

What most people don't know about the bombing, what I don't tell my mother, is that before the car bombs went off, two hand grenades were detonated outside the embassy. Hundreds of people in the surrounding office buildings ran to their windows to see what was going on, then the car bombs exploded. Windows as far as a half-mile away were shattered by the blasts, and hundreds of people were blinded by the splintering glass.

Out on the porch I close my eyes and concentrate on the trickles of sweat running slowly down the sides of my face. The neighborhood is quiet today, no lawn mowers, no radio, no children splashing in a swimming pool. With my eyes still closed I reach out and find my pack of cigarettes. I pull one out and light it and inhale, all in darkness. When it's finished I flick the butt off the porch to my right and imagine it landing in the dirt beneath the arborvitae. On the way through the living room I stumble against a chair and bang my shin. At the entrance to the kitchen I reach out and run my hands along the smooth maple trim and then move on to the cupboard where the glasses are kept. When the ice cubes drop into the glass, I'm startled by the sound, but I keep my eyes closed. I reach into the refrigerator and pull out a pitcher of lemonade and begin pouring it into the glass, listening carefully for the change in pitch that will tell me the glass is full. Then, inexplicably, the pitcher slips from my hand and crashes to the floor at my feet. I open my eyes and look in awe at the shattered remains of the pitcher scattered around my boots like shrapnel.

Then my mother is there. She is there as if she has just materialized from vapor, as if she only exists when there is a reason to exist. As if she feeds on crisis.

"Dear Lord, Scott," she says. "What happened?"

"I broke your pitcher," I say.

It couldn't be much worse. It's a pitcher I've known

my entire life. An antique pitcher of wavy golden glass that was given to her as a wedding gift by her sister. Her sister who shriveled up and died.

I feel immediately ashamed. As if I've let her down. Not just in this moment, but with my entire life. It's all a disappointment. All that potential, gone to waste.

"I'm so sorry," I say, beginning to cry. Something is decalcifying inside me, chipping off in huge flecks. I try to say I'm sorry again, but all I can do is stand there and sob.

My mother looks at me and smiles. There's suddenly a new vitality in her face, the wrinkles around her mouth softened. It's as if this is exactly what she's been waiting for. As if all these years living in the absence of broken glass have been feeding on her like a malignancy.

She raises her hand to my face and pats me on the cheek.

"Don't be silly," she says. "I never liked that pitcher anyway."

"You didn't?" I ask.

"Of course not," she says. "Did you? It was hideous. Now step back and let me get this cleaned up."

My mother is on her knees sweeping shards of golden glass into a dustpan when the telephone rings. She looks up at the phone as if it's something beyond vile, a withered hand pressed between a young girl's thighs. But that shadow quickly passes.

"Get that, will you, Scott?"

"Let's just let it ring," I say.

For a moment she is a little child, innocent,

unspoiled, still capable of feeling wonder. But that shadow passes too.

I don't make her ask again. I move to pick up the phone, but as I do I mutter, "I don't know why you just can't let it ring sometimes."

My mother answers without looking up from her sweeping.

"I'm a pastor's wife, Scott," she says. "I don't have the luxury of ignoring people."

I answer the phone then hold it out to my mother.

"It's Betty Schumacher," I say.

At this my mother stands up and looks at me as if I've just spoken in a foreign language.

"Betty Schumacher," I repeat. "From across the street. What's wrong?"

My mother takes the phone and pauses, covering the mouthpiece with her hand. She stares down at it as if it's the first time she's ever seen one.

"Mom," I urge.

She looks up at me and smiles weakly.

"It's nothing," she says. "It's just that we've been living across the street from one another for twenty-three years, and this is the first time she's ever called me."

As my mother stretches the phone cord into the living room to talk to Betty Schumacher, I work on cleaning up the spill. When I finish, my mother is standing in the kitchen doorway, her face looking a little drained.

"That was Betty Schumacher," she says.

I look at her to see if she's joking, but apparently she isn't.

"She was calling from the hospital," she says. "Her husband cut his hand with his table saw. She had to take him."

She blinks and suddenly looks at me with recognition, as if she's just noticed I'm there.

"Oh, Scott," she says. "Betty's left a cake in the oven. She wants me to take it out. Would you come with me?"

As we cross our quiet, suburban street I feel suddenly vulnerable. I have the sudden urge to hold my mother's hand. It's not something I can initiate. I'm an adult, after all, but I know that if she were to forget my age and out of habit reach for my hand as we stepped off the curb, I would not resist. I would be glad of it.

The inside of the house is darker than ours, and cooler. I have a sudden epiphany: The Schumachers have air conditioning. It then occurs to me that probably everyone on our street has air conditioning. Everyone but my parents.

I want to snoop around, but my mother heads straight for the kitchen and pulls the cake out of the oven. She finds a cooling rack in the first cupboard she tries and sets the cake on top of it.

"Well, that's lucky," she says. "Looks like it's done just right."

She turns off the oven and shuts the door and turns to me.

"Shall we?" she says.

"Go?" I ask.

"Yes, go," she says.

She looks around the kitchen, which is very similar to

hers, except somehow darker, or not as bright, maybe not as clean. All the appliances are from the same era, originally from the sixties, then updated in the eighties. The countertop is the same speckled cream Formica.

"Yes, let's go," she repeats. "It feels strange being in here."

"I'm at least going to check the basement," I say.

"Oh, Scott," she says. "I don't think you should."

"I'll just be a second," I say. "You can head back if you want."

Downstairs it's even cooler. I pass through a paneled rec room with a pool table and a bar, then through a door and into a small woodshop where the light is still on. In the center of the room is a table saw with dots of blood flecked across the blade and fence. I look up and find more blood cast across the dry-walled ceiling, crimson constellations. At my feet, resting in a comfortable bed of braised sawdust, are two fingers, the pinky and ring, still joined together by part of a palm. There is no ring on the ring finger. They are fingers from his right hand.

Upstairs, my mother is still standing in the corner of the kitchen by the oven, as if trying to warm herself. She looks away as I emerge from the basement, already aware that what has happened here is both something gained and something lost.

We have just dropped the fingers into a baggie of ice when the son walks through the door. He is in his late 20s, but still lives at home. I've seen him several times this summer. He drives fast down our quiet street, as if by speeding he could somehow get away.

Before he has a chance to question or accuse, my mother holds the Ziploc bag out in front of her.

"Your father's had an accident, Jimmy," she says. "Your mother's taken him to the hospital."

I'm surprised to hear her so naturally call him by name, but once she's said it I realize that there was a time when I knew it too.

In an instant, and without a word, Jimmy is out the door with the baggie. We hear his tires squeal on the hot pavement as he races away, visions of reattached digits no doubt dancing in his head like sugarplums.

Several days later I awaken much earlier than normal. There's a coolness in the air that I haven't noticed all summer. There's a dewy freshness about the breeze that drifts in the open windows. I can smell flowers and dirt and freshly mown grass, then from the kitchen, freshly brewed coffee. All together it smells like hope.

After putting on my boots and hat and pouring myself a cup of coffee, I walk into the living room and stand at the large French windows that face the road. At the Schumacher's house across the street all the curtains are still drawn. I think about the cool darkness of that house, about what it must feel like to live in there. Would it be comforting to live like that, in all that coolness and dimness, or would it be oppressive?

An image of Betty Schumacher at the hospital pops into my head. She's standing in a well-lit, sterile hallway at a pay phone, frantically leafing through the phone book for my parents' number. I wonder how many other neighbors she tried first, all the ones that she wouldn't have to look up the numbers for. Or was my mother the first? Is there some delineation in her mind between who you call for a cocktail party and who you call when your husband cuts off his fingers?

As I go back to the kitchen for a coffee refill, the sound of breaking glass lures me into the garage. There I find my mother, her back to me, standing in front of a trash can, slowly dropping in each of the eight golden glasses that went with the antique pitcher.

She doesn't notice me as I step out the side garage door and light up a cigarette. I hear the steady hum of a lawn mower, and despite my father's admonition, I walk around to the front of the house, still smoking. Across the street, Jimmy has begun mowing the grass with a riding lawnmower much too large for the size of their lawn. He appears to have the lawnmower in its highest gear, mowing like he drives, fast and angry. On one of his tight turns he looks in my direction and I give him a little nod and tip my hat, but he immediately looks away. I smile and take a drag on my cigarette and polish one of my boots on the back of my pants leg. The sound of breaking glass from inside the garage has stopped. As I toss away the last of the cigarette a fresh breeze blows across the street and I smell something beneath the freshly mown grass, something that could almost be sagebrush—arid and pungent, a mixture of smoke and perfume and blood.

WALKING ON WATER

AT THE END of a nothing winter, the days turn suddenly cold, the mercury plummeting like it's afraid of something, and Janie stands in front of the frosted windows and stares out at the shimmering bay. She paces back and forth, dusting bookshelves and straightening magazines, her hair in the dim living room light like a desert sunset. She rises early now, foregoing those long moments when we would hold each other in bed, our bodies entwined like a willow, not ready to start the day. She is restless, expecting something, and she uses the quiet morning hours to think. I rise with her now and make coffee. I sit at the kitchen table and taste the coffee's bitterness and watch the bay. But Janie won't sit, not for long. She is restless. She paces like a caged animal. She sets her coffee cup down and often, by the time she thinks of it again, discovers that it has grown cold.

I stoke the fire and keep the house warm, but even the fire isn't enough to make Janie sit. She sits for a while, on her mother's couch, the only thing she'd wanted from her parents' house after her mother died. Our hands touch under a blanket pulled over our laps, but then she's over to the window to check on the bay. She stands there with her arms crossed, the wan winter light slanting through the glass and throwing her face into contrast. From where she stands she can see the thermometer, nailed to a fir tree, just at the edge of the deck. It's been below zero for a week now, and Janie knows, we both know, that it's just a matter of time.

It's too cold to go to the job site; the foreman has called off work until the cold snap passes, so I split some wood in the afternoons, although I don't last long. Mostly we are confined to the house, me reading, or tightening the hinges on a cabinet door, and Janie pacing, restless.

One afternoon she puts on her coat, goes out, and starts the car. I'm surprised when it starts, but the sun is shining and that makes a difference. Janie comes back in and lets the car warm up. She stands by the window in her coat and hat and gloves and looks at the bay, which is covered by a thin layer of milky ice.

When she comes back from town I'm sitting in the kitchen with a cup of coffee, working the crossword from the paper. Janie looks at me for a moment, the crossword reminding her of her mother. She has a white Styrofoam container in her hands.

"What's that?" I ask.

"Shiners and chubs," she says.

She puts the container in the refrigerator. Her cheeks are flushed from the cold. She comes over to me and takes my hand.

"Come on," she says, pulling me to my feet. "Come see what I bought."

I put on my coat and boots and Janie leads me out to the car. She opens the trunk, which is spacious, and there I see cases and cases of vintage Orange Crush, the kind in the 10-ounce glass bottles with the painted-on labels, the kind that came, years ago, in wooden crates. I look through the back window and see more stacked in the back seat, more still up front on the passenger side. Some of the crates are worn, their paint fading, but most look brand new.

"How many?" I ask.

"Forty-five cases," she says. "One thousand and eighty bottles."

"Orange Crush," I say.

"When I was little it was the only thing my mother ever drank," says Janie. "In bottles just like this. When it started coming out in cans and plastic, she quit. It wasn't the same anymore."

Janie moves next to me and wraps her mittened

hands around my arm, and we stare together at the
Orange Crush. It's a monument of Orange Crush. A
mandala of Orange Crush. It is, I think, an Orange
Crush shrine.

"Come on," says Janie, dropping my arm. "Let's get
it inside before it freezes."

The next weekend Janie drags me from bed in the
morning and we haul her mother's couch out onto the
ice. The temperature has become seasonal and
temperate, but the numbing cold of the last weeks has
made the ice thick and solid. There are still stars visible
in the morning sky while Janie fools with lines and lures
and I auger through the ice. She puts a Bucktail on the
end of my line and a Swedish Pimple on hers. We sit
back on the couch and put our feet up on the cases of
Orange Crush we've hauled out, our legs covered with a
blanket. We jig with one hand, while holding hands
under the blanket with the other, and when the sun
comes up it's a bright and cloudless day and two eagles
circle above us, hoping to steal our fish. We have a good
spot and we pull out lake trout and whitefish and perch.
Janie takes the first perch and slides it across the ice like
a hockey puck for the eagles. After a while I go back to
the house for sunglasses and sunscreen, and the Hibachi.
We cook the fish right there on the ice and the flaky
meat is hot on our tongues, the Orange Crush cold and
sweet. We slather up with sunscreen, but Janie won't
wear the glasses; she likes the rawness of the light, says
she doesn't want a filter on her world.

Every time Janie finishes an Orange Crush she stands

up and throws the bottle as far as she can. Sometimes they break, but more often they merely clank against the ice and spin away like pinwheels. There's a warm spring-like breeze blowing across the bay and it makes me think that Janie will be happy again, that the grieving will not take something permanently away from her, but may, in fact, only metamorphose her a little, like something fired in a kiln. But it won't happen all at once; it will happen over time, like the approach of a season, and many Orange Crush bottles will have to be broken first.

Janie's mother was driving across the Upper Peninsula when an elk leapt onto the road. She lived long enough for Janie and her brothers to get there, but then she gave them each a faint smile and faded away into death. Janie's brothers hired a lawyer and planned to sue the car company because the airbag had not deployed, but Janie didn't want any part of it. She didn't want to link the memory of her mother with the nastiness of litigation.

"Let it go," she told her brothers.

She stood up at the funeral and told everyone that her mother had been all about love. She told some funny stories and some that made us cry, but mostly she wanted us to know that her mother had been all about love.

"If we all lived like her," she said, "the world would be a better place."

When night falls we leave the couch out on the ice and Janie pulls her nightgown over her head and goes into the bathroom. When she comes out I'm already in bed, tired beyond belief from being out on the ice all day. Janie crawls into bed and slides up next to me.

"I just peed pure Orange Crush," she says.

We both laugh a little and I kiss the top of her head.

"How are your eyes?" I ask.

"Scratchy," she says.

"You'll be blind tomorrow," I say.

"Maybe," she says. "Maybe not."

I fall asleep with Janie nestled against my back and I dream that we're driving through the night, and the sky is pulsing with stars. There's a soft glow in the interior of the car and the radio is playing a sullen tune. We cross a long suspension bridge from one state to another and we notice what looks like Christmas lights everywhere. As we approach the middle of the bridge we realize the lights are from hundreds of little huts and houses on the ice. I stop the car and we get out and stand at the railing of the bridge. As the sky becomes lighter we see that many of the huts have smoke coming from them, but also that there are ATVs and cars and trucks, all on the ice. We realize that we've stumbled on an ice fishing village.

We go down to the ice and walk among the huts and Janie comments that it's more like a city than a village. She walks up to a steel-sided cabin on sleds and opens the door. Inside there's a man in a flannel shirt and insulated pants checking on a pot cooking on the stove. It occurs to me that it's Janie's father, although he died of cancer years ago. The room is warm and full of the smell of food. There's a television tuned to a football game and a small banquet table mounded with snacks and bottles of Orange Crush. Six guys in lounge chairs fish through holes in the carpeted floor. There are burgers and steaks sizzling on a grill, and against one wall, outside the circle of fishermen, is Janie's mother's couch, pale green and forlornly empty. Janie moves to sit on the couch, but as she does there's a thunderish cracking and I look out the door to see that the ice is breaking up. I grab Janie by the hand and we run across the ice, but even as we do I know we won't make it, that we've waited too long. We slip beneath the water, which is warm rather than cold, and we sink and sink, still holding hands.

The next morning Janie is indeed blind. Her eyes are lacquered shut so I wrap them with gauze and we venture back out onto the ice. I reopen the hole and put a maggot on Janie's lure. I've brought a thermos of coffee, but Janie starts in again on the Orange Crush. She drinks them like it's part of a quest or a therapy. It's an Orange Crush fast, a cleansing by sugar and water. She launches the bottles out onto the ice and they pop and rattle in the glaring light. I've put a bell on Janie's tip-up and when it rings she lunges for her line and pulls the fish just to the surface for me to net. She's catching more fish today than yesterday, as if her blindness has heightened her fishing senses.

The next day I go back to work. Before leaving I get Janie situated on the couch, her tip-up rigged with a bell, the cases of Orange Crush within reach. I give her a kiss and tell her I love her, and she tells me that she loves me too. I'm just getting to my truck when I hear the first of the bottles shattering against the ice.

When I get home in the evening I hear gunshots. I walk out onto the deck and look out over the bay, and see that Janie has retrieved my .22 pistol from the top drawer of the bureau. She's dispensed with fishing and has lined up a dozen bottles of Orange Crush twenty or thirty yards away on the ice. She sits cross-legged on the couch and fires rapidly, holding the gun with both hands, her arms outstretched and locked. Mostly she misses, but occasionally there is the pop of a direct hit and the orange eruption of soda like a sunburst. It breaks my heart that she can't see it, the spray of orange, the flowering of the glass, glinting like crushed ice in the setting sun. The gunshots echo back from the mountains across the lake and I feel something roiling in my veins, a splash of ache in my heart. I run to her, my feet skating across the wet ice. I fall over the back of the couch, and I take the gun from her and toss it away. Lying face-up in her lap I hold her face, streaming with tears now, and I say, "Oh Janie. Oh Janie."

On the third day of her blindness Janie is back to fishing. I drink a cup of coffee with her on the couch before going to work. Before I'm done with the coffee she's already pulled three lake trout out of the hole. I throw them on the grill and we listen to the wet skin sizzle. When I leave I kiss her on the forehead and ask her if she's going to be all right.

"Sure," she says. "I'll be fine."

"No more shooting," I say.

"No more shooting," she says.

When I get home from work in the evening Janie is still on the couch fishing. I ask her if she wants to come in, but she says she's not ready. She likes it out on the ice, likes thinking about all that darkness below, and the fish that pass by like shadows. She tells me the ice is a division between two worlds, but that one is just as mysterious as the other. She's nostalgic and mournful, but also strangely content, and I marvel at the role the ice and the fishing and even the Orange Crush have played in the grieving process, because grieving is not just about being sad. It's remembering the good things, and laughing and crying and getting angry, and shooting up bottles of Orange Crush.

As the evening light dims I haul some wood out onto the ice and make a fire that roars and crackles with orange and green flames. The ice around us shifts and moans and Janie and I sit close on the couch, our feet drawn up under the blanket, our arms wrapped around each other. I think about how stubborn Janie is, how stubborn her love is, and I think it will be what saves her, what saves us both.

I reach inside my coat and pull out a flask of whiskey and put it into Janie's hand.

"What's this?" she asks.

"A little warmer upper," I say.

She holds the flask in her lap and doesn't drink.

"I have something to tell you," she says.

I listen to the rise and fall of her breathing, wishing I

could see her eyes. I inhale the scent from the fire as it hisses in a punchbowl of slush.

"You're pregnant," I say.

"Yes," says Janie.

The next day at work I draw a short straw and am relegated to hand digging in a ditch that is twelve feet deep and only two feet wide. Normally a ditch like this is braced with vertical beams wedged in by perpendicular struts to prevent collapse, but the foreman doesn't want to bother with all that; he doesn't want to waste the time or the money. Our project is already several weeks behind schedule because of the cold weather. He sends me down into the ditch with a friendly slap on the back, and I go willingly, because I know I won't be buried alive. Not today. I know this because there's a child waiting for me, a child of my own. I know this because twenty miles away there's a woman fishing the hard water, lashing out in love and anger at bottles of Orange Crush, her love as stubborn as a mule.

It's dark and cool down in the ditch, and I can only see a sliver of sky above, so I'm surprised when I come up at lunch and feel the immediate warm wind of a Chinook. I look around in disbelief. Some of my coworkers have taken off their shirts and their backs are glistening with sweat. I drop the shovel and begin walking, and then running to my truck. As I reach it the foreman shouts to me from across the dirt lot, but I don't respond. My truck fishtails away, a rooster tail of mud in its wake.

The gravel road down to the lake is rutted, the snow

turned to slush. I scare up snowshoe hares and they dart in front of me, zigzagging and disoriented. The daylight is sizzling and there's the smell of things growing, something airborne, and in the field across from our lane I can see green blades of grass pushing up through the pocked snow. The truck skids in front of the garage and I'm out before it has fully stopped. I call Janie's name, the intake of breath a luxury I can't afford, but I see in a snapshot moment that the couch is still there, and that Janie isn't on it.

She is standing on the deck in a fractured octagon of sunlight coming down through the firs. She's wearing a yellow ball gown that had been her mother's, the gauze around her eyes bright white in the sun. When she hears me she turns and smiles, and puts out a hand for me to take.

"I knew you'd be worried," she says.

I kiss her on the neck and we stand at the railing, two people bound by the insistence that we will not let each other go. The ice glistens and heaves and moans, like a creature waking up from a long winter's nap. I touch Janie's cheek and slowly unwrap the bandages from her eyes. When they're off she blinks and touches the lids with the tips of her fingers. She leans her head back against my chest and enjoys this interlude, her Damascene conversion complete.

We watch the eagles circling above the groaning ice, the undersides of their wings glistening like wet slate. We are quiet as the remaining cases of Orange Crush tip like a listing ship and fall through the ice. And we stay put as we hear the muted splintering and moaning and see the nexus of cracks shooting out from the couch like meteors, or falling stars.

PHASE TWELVE

WHEN PERRY SPLITS with Ki I drive down to
Santa Fe to be with him. We've planned a fishing trip up
in the Sangro de Cristos; we're going to fish the streams
up there, way up in the high desert. There's supposed to
be a fish up there, something called a dolphin fish that
will put up a fight like a steelhead. Neither of us has ever
seen one before, but Perry read about it in an airline
magazine he's fond of, and we're going after it.

Perry isn't currently working, although he's had every
job imaginable and we know he'll find another one when
he's ready. He's worked in a pawnshop and a coffee

shop, even a body shop. He's worked as a groundskeeper at a minor league baseball stadium and as a custodian at a dance studio where he spent most of his time polishing the mirrors and emptying the trash cans of tampons. He spent a summer once working at a zoo, using rebar and mesh and cement and plaster to make things that looked like rocks and trees and streambeds. He was a zoo artist. He's also worked at a restaurant where his only task was to make Daiquiris. He spent the whole day slicing lemons and limes and punching the various buttons on the blender. He says all the buttons do the same thing, and he would know. Perry has worked at a driving range, driving that special car that picks up golf balls, and he once wrote an article that was published in *GQ* about the strangest meals you could eat in New York City. For that he ate duck tongue and beef penis and hog intestines. He even ate a guinea pig. In Ecuador a guinea pig is a delicacy, but Perry found it salty and slimy and tough. He doesn't recommend it, even if you're going through an Eat Anything phase. He won't have any trouble finding another job, but first we're going to fish.

It was my wife's idea, this trip to Santa Fe. I'd just buried my father and Nikki thought I needed some time away. I'd been spending a lot of time driving around, just driving, listening to mournful music on the radio, and I wasn't sleeping. Nikki is a doctor, and this was her prescription: a little time away with Perry, good old Perry, just like in the old days. Nikki said it would be good for both of us.

I'd taken care of my father while he died. I gave him

his morphine, his Halcion, his Darvocet, Percocet, Demerol, Zantac, and Prednisone. I tried some of it out myself and especially liked the Percocet. I thought it was like walking through a mirage, the wavy heat rising up from baking sand. I bathed my father and put lotion on his bedsores and shared his drugs. I kissed him on the forehead each morning when he awoke and each evening when he fell asleep, although it was an effort, because his skin tasted like death. It wasn't a good way to die, this wasting away from the inside like a decaying piece of fruit, and I needed to get it out of my system. I needed to get focused back on life, not death, and a little time with Perry was just the thing to do it.

This isn't the first time that Perry and Ki have split. Their marriage is like a smoldering volcano, hot and intense, and sometimes it erupts. Their fights are the kind that require a trip to Wal-Mart afterward, to replace all the things they've broken. Perry has shown me scars from these fights, raised up and pink on his hands, his back, at his hairline. They both have scars. They once split up because Perry didn't feed Ki's cat. He fed his cat, but not Ki's. She came home from a business trip and threw a twenty-pound bag of cat food through the kitchen window. Then she stormed out and stayed away for three days, without taking the cat with her, which makes no sense. When Ki leaves she goes to her sister's who lives only ten minutes away, so it's almost like not leaving at all. Sometimes they talk on the phone and when Ki comes back Perry mixes up a batch of Cuba Libres, and they act like nothing's happened.

One morning early, I kiss Nikki good-bye. She runs her hand through my hair and hands me a thermos of coffee. She's worried about me driving, because I haven't been sleeping, and makes me promise to pull over or get a motel if I'm tired. I promise and kiss her again. Then I put the thermos on the passenger seat and drive.

While I drive I think about when Perry and Ki first met. I was there at the time so in a way I've been a part of their marriage from the very beginning. Perry was in his cowboy phase at the time. He was wearing alligator skin boots and a bolo tie. He was wearing designer cologne that smelled like a saddle. It may have been called Saddle. We were living in Boulder at the time, supposedly in graduate school, but in reality we mostly fished and drank exotic drinks like Cuba Libres, which are made with rum and diet Coke and lime juice. We slept in late and went out to breakfast in little diners and ordered biscuits and gravy and coffee. Sometimes we would drive down to the airport and drink in one of the airport bars. The drinks were expensive and watered down, but nobody thought ill of you if you ordered a drink before noon. In fact, they expected it.

We met Ki in one of the airport bars. It was around twelve o'clock, but I don't know if it was noon or midnight. We sat down and put our elbows on the bar, and soon the bartender came over and put napkins down in front of us. She was short and pretty, and had a nose that turned up a little at the end giving you the impression that she was always on the verge of saying something. Her eyes had a little sadness that pooled at the corners, but she wasn't really a sad person. When she turned away we both watched her backside, which was quite lovely. Perry leaned over to me and told me he was planning to marry the bartender, and I agreed that it wouldn't be such a bad thing to do.

When she came back with the drinks (we were drinking Sidecars at the time) Perry slipped into a western twang and said, "I'll bet you're from Abilene." Something about this made Ki snort. She must have found his off-kilter approach both disarming and attractive. Soon she was drinking Sidecars with us and the coppery overhead lighting and the distant sound of the boarding calls made us all feel that anything was possible.

I haven't had a Sidecar now in years. But I think when I get to Santa Fe, Perry and I will have to go out and have one. Maybe we'll even go to the airport. We'll sit at the airport bar and drink Sidecars and remember the good times. We'll remember that midnight or noon when we first met Ki, and how we ended up not having to pay for the drinks because she was the bartender and she was already in love with him. Yes, we'll drink Sidecars and remember. But first, we'll fish.

Perry and I also like drinking in hotel bars. Once we were drinking in a hotel bar in Denver where there was a lawyer's convention. This was during Perry's vegan phase. The bar was large and had a glass ceiling, and it was full of lawyers. The lawyers were drinking and talking loudly, and telling sexist jokes. A couple of the lawyers tried to get us to join them, but we weren't interested. We just sat at the bar and talked to the bartender who wasn't especially pretty, but who was on our side because she didn't like the lawyers either. That night we were drinking Jamaican punch, which is made with gin and rum, but also has tea in it. They were eight dollars apiece and we'd lost count of how many we'd had, but we didn't care. We were charging everything to room 212, even though we weren't staying there. We knew one of the lawyers would end up paying, probably without even noticing.

Later in the evening we started telling lawyer jokes. Between Perry and me and the bartender we knew almost every lawyer joke in the world. At first the lawyers thought it was funny and we were all laughing together, laughing so hard we were crying, but then one of the lawyers realized that we weren't laughing with them but at them and he grabbed Perry by the front of the shirt and reared back with his fist.

"Stop! Stop!" cried the bartender. "He's a vegan!"

Somehow this had a placating effect on the lawyer and he let go of Perry's shirt and smoothed out the wrinkles.

Out in the parking lot I said, "Stop! He's a vegan!" and Perry laughed so hard that he fell against someone's car and made the alarm go off.

When I get down to Santa Fe I'll say it to him again. I'll say, "Stop! He's a vegan!" and Perry won't be able to control himself. He'll laugh so hard his eyes will water and maybe he'll even soil himself.

But I won't do that when I first get there. First, we'll

go fishing. We'll go after the elusive dolphin fish, a fish that even Hemingway never caught.

I once saw Perry ride a cow. Ironically this was not during his cowboy phase. He was, I believe, between phases at the time, but I suppose you could say he was in a transitional phase. It was a steer actually, but Perry has always referred to it as a cow. We were mountain biking in Eldorado Canyon when we saw a lone steer on the trail in front of us. When he heard us coming he started trotting up the trail, but Perry stood up in his pedals and soon caught up. He got right up alongside the steer and they ran together for a while like that, like it was Pamplona. I don't think the steer knew what to think of him. There was barely enough room for the two of them in the narrow canyon. Then Perry threw a leg over his bike and jumped onto the steer's back. He grabbed onto the horns and rode him up the canyon, bouncing around like a rag doll. They were going so fast I couldn't keep up and after a while I lost sight of them. Then the steer came running back down the trail and passed me, and Perry was nowhere in sight. I found him between two sandstone boulders bleeding from the head, but he wasn't as bad off as he looked. He was able to laugh about it immediately. When we're together in Santa Fe in some hotel bar drinking Singapore slings Perry will remember. He'll look at himself in the mirror behind the bar and he'll see the serrated scar on his forehead and he'll remember. He'll look at me with that half-smile, half-smirk of his and he'll say, "Remember when I rode that cow?"

Perry didn't ask Ki to marry him in an airport bar. It wasn't a hotel bar either. It was a sushi bar! They'd just finished a plate of baby octopus and were moving on to some smoked eel, when Perry said, "Let's get hitched."

Ki, with her mouth full of rice and eel said, "Where should we do it?"

"On top of Mount Kilimanjaro," said Perry.

"On a beach in Vietnam," said Ki.

"Death Valley," said Perry.

"The Panama Canal," said Ki.

Right away Perry moved into his weight-loss phase. He gave up carbs, then he gave up fat, then he gave up eating all together. He went six weeks without having a bowel movement and his skin hung off him like a yellowed toga. His ribs protruded like thorny rose stalks. Ki threatened to leave him, so he went on a juice fast, which wasn't exactly what she'd been hoping for, but it was enough to make her stay.

During this time Perry experienced an almost euphoric clarity of mind. Toward the end of the weight-loss phase he invented a fabric made from recycled milk jugs and thus transitioned smoothly into his inventor phase. The fabric was warm and soft and wicked moisture away from your skin. He and Ki sewed the fabric into garments and sold them at the local farmers' market, but Perry neglected to get a patent and soon the stuff was showing up in Patagonia catalogs. This was disappointing enough to send him right into his reptile phase. During this phase he went out to the desert and caught snakes and lizards and put them in Tupperware containers with little holes poked in the lids. His skin became tough and scaly and his eyes were like a cobra's. I thought this would be enough to drive any woman away, but Ki didn't object; she was just happy the weight-loss phase had ended.

For a long weekend during the inventor phase I stayed with Perry. Ki was out of town on another business trip and he wanted the company. We went over to his parents' house who were in Vermont for the summer and raided his father's vast liquor cabinet. All weekend we sat out by the pool drinking the drinks that Perry invented. He made drinks that no one had ever heard of before and we gave them names that no one would ever hear again. He made a Pilot's Demise, and a Shirtless Girlfriend, and a Truncated Haiku. He made a purple concoction that we dubbed a Three-day Bruise and a red mixture that we called O Positive. The O Positive turned out to be my favorite. All weekend we sat by the pool and when Perry wasn't mixing new drinks he was talking about his love for Ki. He went on and on about how much he loved her, how it was an ethereal thing, something beyond his control or comprehension.

"Stop it," I said. "You're making me sick. Make me another O Positive!"

Perry has been through eleven phases that I'm aware of. As I drive toward Santa Fe, I remember. In addition to the ones I've mentioned there was the Samurai warrior phase, the pheromone phase, and the dead poets phase. There was also a brief nudity phase during which Ki also threatened to leave him because she was having to do all the shopping. And, oh yes, the airline magazine phase, which I never fully understood, but which Ki was quite tolerant of.

Eleven phases and all of them entered into with such passion and vigor and no fear of regret. As I drive, I remember and think. What will I find when I get to Santa Fe? Will it be a tai chi phase? A bowling league phase? Perhaps a Greenpeace phase or a ballroom dancing phase? I'm looking forward to finding out. Whatever it is it will be dynamic and spirited and full of heart. For now I think of it only as Phase Twelve, but soon it will have another name. Perry and I will fish and we'll give this new phase a name. We'll drink in airport bars and hotel bars, and we'll find new places to drink, places no one has ever thought to drink before. And then we'll fish some more, high up in the Sangro de Cristos. We'll fish for the elusive dolphin fish, and when we catch it we'll either eat it or set it free, all depending on our mood at the moment.

ANGELS DON'T SLEEP

THE WORST JOB I ever had was walking Mrs. X's dogs, but it was the job that introduced me to Jeff, and for that I'm grateful.

Jeff had an Akita that was an angel. I don't mean that the dog was well-behaved and good. I mean actually an angel, a celestial being, one of the heavenly host, come to earth incarnate as a dog to teach us that there is wonder and mystery in the world, that the free gift of grace is available to us, that God chooses to be among us, if we just have eyes to see it. At least that's what Jeff claimed.

I know that people are given to moments when everything is altered for them, key instances when a word or a look or a wayward galvanic notion cements that nothing will be exactly the same again. For me it was the chance encounter with Jeff and his dog, Raphael. But maybe chance had nothing to do with it.

Mrs. X had three Corgis, a breed that is amiable and cute, but has manic herding instincts and doesn't know how to wipe itself. I took them to the park every weekday at noon where I would let them off their leads and watch them herd the squirrels and ducks and other dogs. Mrs. X made me take them whatever the weather, but mostly it was nice and I could sit on a park bench and read. It really wasn't a terrible job, but I was grieving and feeling insignificant, aimless and generally bad about myself at the time, so I naturally transferred these emotions to my employment.

A year earlier I'd had everything figured out. I was going to spend the summer working as an editorial intern at *The Garden City Review* then start graduate school in the fall. But a week before my internship was to start my parents were both killed in a car accident and I spent the summer putting their affairs in order and drinking screwdrivers for breakfast every morning. By the end of the summer it was clear even to me that I was in no shape for graduate school. I'd closed all my parents' accounts and paid off the outstanding debts. But I hadn't bothered to pay the phone and I only paid the power bill once all summer, but it was enough to keep it turned on so I still had ice for my screwdrivers. I hadn't decided what to do with the house. I didn't want it, but selling it seemed more than I was capable of. I sat in my parents' drab olive kitchen one morning toying with an untoasted English muffin and sipping a screwdriver that was more vodka than orange juice when I spied Mrs. X's ad in the paper.

I read the ad over then looked out the window where a garbage truck had stopped between our driveway and the neighbor's. I watched as a lanky young man with unkempt hair dumped the neighbor's garbage into the truck then replaced the cans neatly on the lawn. I hadn't put out any garbage in weeks because I wasn't generating any, but the young man still walked over to the foot of the driveway and lingered there a moment, as if he was uncertain what to do. He glanced up at the kitchen window and brushed the hair away from his eyes. I gave him a little wave, but there must have been a glare on the window because he didn't react. I was thinking, *C'mon in. Take a load off. I've got nothing better to do.* But the truck started moving and Mr. Lean and Lanky jumped on the back and they moved down the street with him holding on with one hand, his other hand hanging casually at his side in a way that I thought was overtly sexual. I was left staring at the neighbor's empty trash cans. I really should be generating a little garbage, I thought. Something more than orange juice cartons and bottles of vodka. If not for myself, then for the nice garbage man. I couldn't help thinking he was a little disappointed with me.

The next day Mrs. X met me at the door and looked

me over. She must have been satisfied because she allowed me into the tiled foyer and began explaining my duties, which was walking the dogs for two hours every day and occasionally picking up some groceries. She ate only organics and shopped one day at a time so everything would be fresh. Her husband was dead, her children were grown and gone, and she was working on a translation of a Portuguese book of poetry that had been written, as far as anyone could figure, around 1500 A.D. She'd gotten the Corgis after her husband died, but almost immediately began regretting it.

"What was I thinking?" she said as she handed me the leads. She had gray hair, which she wore up, fastened with pins, but it was always half undone, charcoal wisps of it falling over her face and constantly getting pushed aside. "I thought they'd be nice companions, but it's like having three toddlers in the house again. They're really quite annoying."

That they were. They bounced on top of each other and barked and yelped and continually got tangled up in their leads. They always had a smear of shit on their backsides and if it was raining their bellies quickly took on the look of a piece of fleece dragged through a cesspool. But once at the park, I could let them go. They'd run in manic widening circles in search of something to herd and if they couldn't find anything they'd herd each other, although it was never very clear how that was working.

I walked Mrs. X's dogs all winter, my disdain for them escalating until the days started growing longer.

Then my disdain slowly leveled off into disinterested apathy. I was still medicating myself with screwdrivers in the mornings, but I was also throwing out the occasional pizza box for the garbage man, which I rationalized as a sign of emotional health. I was, after all, thinking of someone besides myself.

Jeff and Raphael walked into the park on a spring day that was bright and warm, but to me seemed dull and matted. Spring was when my mother would spend hours on her knees in the garden, cleaning the beds of last year's detritus around the perennials and planting flat after flat of annuals that burst forth in reds and yellows and oranges and blues. She always wore a wide-brimmed straw hat to keep the sun off her face and I thought it made her look like she was from another era, although I couldn't have said which one.

Jeff's sweater, the blue of it, reminded me of my mother's delphiniums. I was sitting on a bench not really reading my book when he and Raphael emerged from the trees on the far side of the park. They walked across the rolling lawns, together, and yet not exactly together, both of their noses turned slightly up to the breeze, as if on the lookout for something. I was mesmerized by the two of them. I felt an electric tingling at the back of my neck, something similar between my legs. I pushed my sunglasses up on my nose and watched them make their way across the bright green grass. He wasn't especially attractive, not in the angular, sinewy, mussed hair garbage man way. It was more his substance I noticed, his largeness, the way he looked at the world, seeing everything and absorbing it.

The Corgis noticed them soon enough, streaking and yelping across the lawn, intent on corralling them, their myopia impressive, containment their sole objective. I was worried for a moment about how Raphael would react to this onslaught. He was massive, his powerful jaws capable of snapping the Corgis' backs like dry twigs, but as the dogs approached he merely sat, and the Corgis were so taken aback by this maneuver that they were completely befuddled, something I wouldn't have thought possible. Their reaction, however, was even more amazing. When they'd approached to within about ten feet they suddenly stopped and, mimicking Raphael, respectfully sat.

I left my book on the bench and went over, feeling for the first time something I hadn't felt since my parents' death, although I couldn't have said what it was, only that it was new, and I suppose, welcomed. Jeff stood several yards away from the dogs' strange tableau, not noticing, or not thinking anything unusual about it, but when I approached he turned and smiled. For a moment I looked into his cactus green eyes, but then I found myself focusing on a spot below his chin.

"Is this your dog?" I asked.

Jeff laughed and held up his hands.

"Maybe," he said. "Or maybe I'm his human."

Normally this kind of pantywaist sentimentality would have made me nauseous, but the way Jeff said it was so unaffected, as if it had never occurred to him that Raphael might be his dog, as if they hadn't yet figured out what their relationship was to each other. He noticed me staring at him and took a step closer.

"I'm Jeff."

He looked at me as if I might need clarification, as if a simple introduction of first names might be beyond my ability. Was I acting strange? Had I lost the capacity for dialogue?

"And this," he said, indicating his dog, "is Raphael."

At this Raphael turned his attention away from the Corgis for the first time and looked at me. For a moment he seemed to be sizing me up, but then his eyes narrowed and he blinked with compassion.

"Hello, Raphael," I said.

I turned back to Jeff who was removing his sweater and tying it around his waist. The sky was a radar blue and the park was suddenly full of the scent of pine, the chirping of birds, the sound of children's laughter, the faraway gurgling of the stream that bisected the park. I tucked my hair behind an ear and felt a slow pulsing. I wanted him to kiss me. I needed him to. I hadn't been touched by another human being since my parents' death, since that awful afternoon when strangers streamed into my parents' house carrying casseroles that piled up on the kitchen counters like debris at a demolition site. I desperately wanted his lips on mine. But I knew at the same time it was wrong, that I'd be flirting with something I didn't fully understand or deserve. I shoved my hands into my jeans and looked down at Raphael.

"How does he do that?"

Jeff looked at the dogs and gave a little shrug.

"Raphael is an angel. I imagine your dogs are impressed."

"They're not my dogs," I said.

As soon as it was out of my mouth I realized how belligerent it sounded. Why was I being combative? Was it because my parents were dead? Because all my plans were spoiled and I was alone and miserable and it would be a dishonor to their memories if I started to feel otherwise?

"How do you know he's an angel?" I tried.

Jeff looked at me for a long moment, his head slightly cocked. He had crow's feet at the corners of his eyes, like a freshly plowed field.

"Raphael has taught me to see things. To notice things."

"What kind of things?"

Jeff kept staring at me and I forced myself to hold his gaze.

"Like the sorrow in your eyes," he said.

I looked at him for a moment then looked over his shoulder to the edge of the woods where two boys were fighting with swords, which were really sticks. I crossed my arms over my chest. I didn't feel like crying, but all the emotion of the last year came rising up. I wanted to die or to leave, but I had nowhere to go. Why was I still living in my parents' house with the phone turned off? I looked back at Jeff's green eyes.

"My parents died last year," I said. "I have vodka for breakfast."

This statement seemed to visibly cause him pain, but he didn't reach out to touch me like I hoped he might. He turned his face into the wind and took a deep breath, and nodded.

"My parents are dead, too," he said.

Please don't say, *But they're in a better place*, I thought. But he didn't. He just looked at me in the way he did that made me feel like something was gurgling inside me and asked if I liked coffee.

Coffee, I thought. Yes, coffee. It seemed like a foreign word, like a word from a language I'd once known but had forgotten.

"I love coffee," I said.

"I know a place that makes the best coffee on the planet," he said. "Will you be here tomorrow?"

"I'm here every day."

"I'll bring you some."

He smiled and ran his hand through his hair, which I noticed was really more white than blond. Then Raphael suddenly stood up and began walking toward the woods, and Jeff followed. I watched until they disappeared. Then I looked at the Corgis who were still sitting, but were now looking at me for direction.

"That big dog was an angel," I said, as if that explained everything.

Since my parents' death I'd been sleeping on the living room couch, unable to fall asleep without the TV, but that night, after fixing myself a screwdriver, I wandered into their room. It was thick with a dim light that hung in the air like gauze. I ran my finger over the surface of their bureau and snaked a trail through the accumulated dust. I picked up one of my mother's earrings and held it up to my ear in front of her mirror. I had never thought we'd looked much alike, but now in the muted light, with all the weight I'd lost, I looked much older, and thought I saw a resemblance. A dog barked somewhere in the neighborhood. I ran my hand over the quilted bedspread and sat on the edge of the bed. When I finished my screwdriver I lay back and fanned out my arms, and closed my eyes.

I dreamed that my parents had gone to a foreign country, a country I didn't recognize. On one of their excursions they rented horses and rode high into the mountains along a river that glittered in the sunlight. After a while they could see faces beneath the surface of the water and the horses had turned into bridleless dogs. They turned away from the river and crossed a razor-stubbled cornfield, like a sheet of gold. The dogs ran side by side, their gait so even that it was possible for my parents to hold hands. Their silhouettes got smaller and smaller until at last they vanished in a burst of golden light.

I awoke and imagined that Jeff and Raphael were in the room. I thought I heard Raphael's quiet breathing somewhere in the corner.

"Are you there?" I said.

I waited and found myself trying to conjure Jeff's appearance. When I was with him I hadn't thought much about what he looked like. But now in the darkness it was hard to remember his physical being at all, except that he was large, in the sense that he took up space. But whether this was with his physical being or just what he projected emotionally and spiritually was hard to say.

I fell back to sleep and dreamed that I quit on Mrs. X. I was dreading doing it, but knew I had to. I had to be free of her and those stupid dogs. I walked to her house and for some reason I had the dogs with me. They tugged at the leads and pulled in different directions and got so tangled that I had to unfasten them to get them straightened out. We took several wrong turns and walked down streets I didn't recognize, but then at last I spotted her house and went up and knocked on the door. I didn't know how she would react. She had come to count on me and I didn't want to let her down, but I had to make her understand that I couldn't do it anymore. But when she opened the door I saw that she was holding the book she'd been working on. It was already published, bound in Manila cloth with gold lettering. She held it out to me and I took it, trading her for the dogs.

The next morning someone was knocking at my door. I pulled myself out of bed and noticed that I was still wearing my clothes from the day before. I stumbled down the hall and into the kitchen. The knocking continued, but I took the time to pour myself a quick screwdriver. Who could it be, anyway? No one even knew I existed. I took a long sip then pulled back the curtain and saw Jeff and Raphael standing on the front porch with the morning sun pouring down on them like a spotlight.

I opened the door and Jeff produced a steaming cup of coffee.

"I didn't think you'd want to wait until noon for this," he said.

I took the coffee but couldn't think what to say. Raphael sat down on the porch facing the street. Jeff just stood there.

"How did you know where I lived?" I asked.

Jeff smiled.

"Raphael knew," he said.

There was a slight southerly breeze. A strand of hair blew across my face and stuck between my lips. I brushed it away and tucked it behind an ear. I looked at the coffee. It smelled nice. It had been a long time since I'd had coffee.

"Do you want to come in?" I asked.

Jeff looked up at the indigo sky and squinted.

"I'm not much of an inside person," he said.

"No," I said. The coffee was warm in my hands. "And I don't suppose Raphael is much of an inside dog."

Jeff laughed.

"No," he said. "Even in the coldest weather he prefers to sleep outside instead of at the foot of my bed."

Something about this statement seemed strange to me. I took a sip of the coffee, which was thick and strong and had the faint hint of some spice I couldn't identify. I stepped out onto the porch and sat down next to Raphael, and ran my hand through the thick fur at the back of his neck. Jeff sat down next to me and put his forearms on his knees.

"Beautiful day," he said.

That it was. The grass was green and the sky was blue and the air was warm and sweet. The trees that lined the street were filled with small brown birds that chirped and flashed from branch to branch. There was a soft salmon sunlight that warmed my shoulders. Across the street in the neighbor's yard I saw a bunny appear from beneath a bush and nibble the green grass. I experienced one of those flashes of insight when everything seems absurd—when all your troubles, all your worries, all your hopelessness, suddenly seem trivial and overblown. I started to quietly cry, which did not seem to disconcert Jeff and Raphael in the least. They were good company. They gazed across the street, their noses slightly raised, taking everything in. When I'd stopped crying Raphael gave my cheek a single lick with his coarse tongue then dropped down with his chin between his paws.

"How much does he weigh?" I asked.

Jeff looked at Raphael seriously, as if he'd never considered the question.

"With or without the wings?" he said at last.

"I don't see any wings," I said.

Jeff was about to laugh, but then he stopped himself.

"Yes," he said. "Well, the wings don't weigh much."

We watched as a boy on a bike coasted down the middle of the street. I wanted Jeff to kiss me. I wondered if he ever would. I wanted the two of them to move in, so I could always feel this way. Jeff looked at me, the lines of his face soft in the morning light. I thought he could tell what I was thinking.

"How's your sorrow?" he asked.

"I don't notice it so much when I'm with you two," I said.

I took a sip of the coffee. The spice seemed to be growing stronger. I ran my fingers through my hair and took a breath.

"It's been a long time since I've let myself feel anything," I said. "Things other than anger and bitterness and disillusionment, the feeling of being betrayed and left. I haven't had a cup of coffee in a year."

"Do you like it?" he asked.

"Very much."

Jeff looked across the street. The bunny had ventured into the middle of the lawn, farther from the protection of the bushes.

"Have I ever told you about the Human Fly?"

I suddenly missed my mother terribly. I wished she were here, so I could share Jeff and Raphael with her. Isn't he peculiar? I'd say to her. The way he phrases things. Like that question, like he's known me for years.

I touched Raphael's soft, warm fur and looked down at my bare feet.

"I don't think you have," I said.

"His name was George Gibson Polley. When he was a boy in Richmond, Virginia, one day he hit a baseball onto the roof of a six-story building. Since it was the only ball they had, he climbed up to get it. They went back to playing, but for the rest of the game George was distracted. Climbing that building had stirred something inside him. In 1910 his family moved to Chicago, and George got a job as a newspaper boy. One day he saw an expensive suit in a store window. 'I'd stand on my head on top of this building for a suit like that,' he declared. The store owner heard him and laughed. 'If you did that, I'd give you the suit,' he said."

I looked at Jeff's profile, but kept stroking Raphael's fur. I had a feeling he was talking about himself.

"What happened?" I asked.

"George got the suit. And a career. The episode attracted so much attention that a local theater offered him a booking. He climbed buildings to attract crowds to the show."

The coffee was making my head buzz a little. The air was full of the smell of honeysuckle from the neighbor's yard. Raphael rolled over and let me scratch his belly.

"He became known as the Human Fly," Jeff continued. "He climbed buildings all over the country. In Boston he climbed 500 feet up the Custom House; in Hartford he scaled three buildings in one day; in New York he climbed the Woolworth Building—in 1920 the tallest building in the world. Part of his act was to pretend to slip and fall; he would suddenly drop from one ledge to another never failing to make the crowd gasp. By the time he was 29 he'd climbed 2,000 buildings without a fall."

Jeff stopped, looking back in time. A car drove past, stirring up some debris from the gutter.

"What happened?" I asked. The story was making me angry. Why would someone needlessly take such risks with his life? What is this need for danger and attention? Did the Human Fly ever think about the people who loved him?

Jeff looked at me and for the first time I saw what must have been there all along—my sorrow reflected in his eyes.

"He fell, right?" I said.

The breeze blew warmly across the porch and Jeff scratched at something on his lip.

"He never fell. He died of a brain tumor."

That night I again woke in the middle of my parents' bed. The house was quiet and cool, and there was the soft patter of spring rain outside. After a few minutes of staring at the invisible ceiling I knew I wouldn't be able to fall back to sleep. I kept thinking about Jeff's story. What was the point? That life was random? That terrible things happened? That it was all out of our control? What had he been trying to tell me?

I went to the kitchen where I discovered that the power was out. I flipped the kitchen light switch several times, as if repetition might be the solution. After a while I went into the living room and sat on the couch, and stared at the blank television. I pulled my nightgown up and touched the smooth skin of my knees. I thought about Jeff and Raphael walking away down the street together, the morning sunlight making the air around their shoulders glow. I thought about the Human Fly who continually defied death only to be struck down by something inside his own body. I got up and wandered around the dark house, realizing I knew the layout of walls and furniture so well that I had no need of the lights. I went to my old room, which smelled of the perfume I used to wear as a young teenager. I stood there for a long time, thinking of my life not as a path, but something else, something that fanned out in several directions at once. I knew it was wrong to think of the Human Fly as selfish and inconsiderate. His death was not something he orchestrated. His death was not something he did to someone else.

I went back to my parents' room and picked up their wedding picture from the bureau. I wiped my hand across the glass and a single tear fell onto my mother's face.

"I know it wasn't your fault," I said. "I know you didn't leave me."

For a long time I stood at the window. I could see the rain slanting through the glow of a streetlight halfway down the street. For a moment I let myself wonder where Jeff and Raphael were sleeping, but then I caught myself. Because I knew that people like that didn't sleep.

NORMAL LIKE US

DAN WAS IN THE BACKYARD fixing drinks. Dan could make just about anything, but this was summer, and in the summer his specialty was gin and tonics. Dan's gin and tonics were sublime. He said it was because he made them with love, but the truth is he used a very fine gin from London that he kept in the freezer, and he insisted on those small bottles of tonic water made by Canada Dry. The small bottles were essential because they prevented the tonic from ever having a chance to go flat. The other key ingredient was the limes. Dan always had the freshest limes with deep green rinds like the skin of a newborn crocodile. And, he never cut them ahead of time. The mistake some people make is squeezing too much lime juice over the ice before making the drink, but Dan never did. If you watched him, you could see the trick. He gave the wedge of lime just the slightest squeeze, until the finest mist of juice came out, before dropping the wedge into the glass. He made it look easy, but of course not everybody could do it. Dan's gin and tonics were legendary, throughout the neighborhood and beyond. I've been all over and I've never had one that compared.

It was the Fourth of July and if anything Dan was making his gin and tonics even better than usual. At first it was just Dan and me and the wives, but after a while a guy named Steve showed up. I didn't know Steve very well. He was someone who worked with Dan. I'd met him a time or two, but I didn't really know him. It irritated me a little that Steve had shown up. I know he'd been invited, but didn't he have somewhere else to go on the Fourth of July? I was afraid that he and Dan would start talking about work and then the wives and I wouldn't have anything to say. We'd be the outsiders.

When Steve arrived Dan was standing behind his new bar. It was one of those foldout faux teak things they sell at the Coast to Coast for two hundred bucks. It had an umbrella that slid down into a hole in the middle of the bar and provided shade while you fixed drinks. Dan was standing there mixing me a fresh gin and tonic when Steve arrived. At first Steve stood right there at the bar watching Dan fix my drink. The rest of us were sitting in wicker chairs several yards away on the grass, but Steve was right there with Dan. If Dan had reached out his arm he could have touched Steve on the chin. I didn't know why he had to stand right there at the bar. I didn't want Steve there with Dan, talking about work, maybe distracting him from the job at hand. So far all the gin and tonics had been exemplary and I didn't want to have to experience the first one that wasn't up to par. But after a few minutes, with his own drink in hand, Steve moved away from the bar and started talking to Dan's wife. She knew him better than I did, because of course, Dan worked with him. They'd probably had him over for dinner fifty times.

Dan had a nice yard. It was a good place for a party. It was private and nicely landscaped. There were some red and purple flowers in a raised bed along the back fence, although they'd been on their way out for a couple of weeks. The day was heating up. There were little waves of heat rising from the patio stones. I looked over at my wife and asked her how she was feeling. She was over eight months pregnant and looked like she was hiding a keg of beer under her smock.

"I'm okay," she said, but I could tell she was uncomfortable. Her face was red and blotchy, and I knew she was wishing she could have one of Dan's gin and tonics.

I heard Steve talking to Dan's wife. I heard him tell her that his own wife had gone to the coast for a family reunion. When Dan's wife asked him why he hadn't gone along all Steve said was, "I dunno," as if that explained everything.

The plan was to roast some hotlinks on the grill, but so far no one seemed inclined to get it going. It was hot and the gin and tonics were going down as easily as could be. It was a good party, even without the hotlinks. Everyone was enjoying themselves, even my wife, although I could tell she was thinking about those gin and tonics. She was a good-looking woman, even eight months pregnant, and I was proud that she was my wife. I doubted really if Steve actually had a wife. He could have been making the whole family reunion business up.

Dan made fresh drinks for everyone. My wife was drinking iced tea with thick wedges of lemon in it. Dan finally sat down in a chair next to his wife. I thought he and Steve would start talking about work, but just then the next-door neighbor poked her head over the fence. I'd met this neighbor once or twice before when I'd been over at Dan's backyard. She was tall and thin, and she had sinewy arms. I thought she might have a little Native American in her. Maybe some Sioux or Chippewa. She looked like she might. She had a little girl that there was something wrong with. I couldn't remember what it was. A birth defect or a brain tumor, I couldn't remember. Anyway this neighbor poked her head over the fence and said, "What's this? A party?"

"Sure," piped up Steve. "Sure it's a party. Why don't you join us?"

It was none of Steve's business inviting this woman to the party. It wasn't something Dan or any of the rest of us had any problem with. We were glad to have the neighbor woman over. It just wasn't Steve's business and I always found it a little annoying when people overstepped their business. Steve was always doing that. He didn't know when to stop.

The woman's head disappeared from above the fence and in a few moments the gate at the side of the house opened and she came through it. She had her little girl with her. At first I thought I'd been mistaken, that I'd remembered wrong, because there didn't seem to be anything wrong with her. She was wearing a cute flowered dress with white sandals. I thought maybe I'd had it all wrong. But when she got closer I saw what it was. There was something wrong with her upper lip. It was swollen and curled up, and it was a little discolored, like fruit that's starting to go bad. It looked like she'd fallen against something, banged herself up, but it wasn't from an accident. It wasn't from swelling. It was like that all the time. It'd been like that since she'd been born. It was too bad, because she was otherwise a very pretty little girl. I thought she'd be a real beauty, except for the lip.

The two of them came into our circle and the introductions were made. The woman's name was Georgia and the little girl's name was Anna. I thought she looked like an Anna, that it was a good name for her. But I couldn't help staring at her lip. Without it I think she would have been one of the prettiest girls I'd ever seen. I wondered if anything could be done about it. Some kind of corrective surgery. I was sure there was. Maybe they were just waiting until she was a little older.

Or maybe they didn't have the money. Insurance never seemed to cover things like that.

No one else seemed to be bothered by the girl's lip. Not even Steve. I suppose they were used to it. They'd probably seen her a thousand times.

Of course Dan jumped up and offered to make Georgia a gin and tonic.

"That's what we're drinking," he said. "Gin and tonics on the Fourth of July."

Georgia agreed.

"That sounds just right," she said. "I think I'd like a gin and tonic very much."

I wanted to say something smart. I wanted to show Georgia that I wasn't bothered by her daughter's lip, but all I could think to say was, "Dan makes the best gin and tonics."

It was probably not the right thing to say. She was Dan's next-door neighbor after all. She'd probably had his gin and tonics before. She probably knew better than I did how good they were.

But Georgia smiled at me anyway. She knew it wasn't a very smart thing to say, but she was gracious. She didn't want to make me feel bad.

After Dan was finished making Georgia a gin and tonic, he looked at Anna who had been standing right next to her mother the whole time.

"What about you, young lady?" asked Dan. "Lemonade? Iced tea?"

The little girl looked up at her mother.

"Anything you want," Georgia said.

"Lemonade, please," said Anna.

She was a polite little girl. I could see that. And that lip didn't seem to get in the way of how she talked. She said *Lemonade, please* just like any girl her age would. But perhaps a little more politely. A lot of girls her age wouldn't be that polite.

While Dan poured Anna a glass of lemonade, I went into the house to use the bathroom. Inside the house it was cool. I could hear the air conditioner churning away. The bathroom was down a long hallway where the bedrooms were. I noticed that the walls of the hallway were lined with framed pictures. Most of the pictures were of Dan's kids, starting as little babies, then through the years as they got older. They were all in high school now. Dan told me that they'd gone with some friends and were having a picnic down at the lake. They were going to go swimming and grill hamburgers on a barbecue. They'd probably find a way to get some beer, Dan said, but he wasn't worried. They were good kids. He said he'd done the same thing when he was a kid and I admitted that I had too. I looked at the pictures and realized that my wife and I had all that in front of us. Dan already had a family. We were just starting ours.

Back outside my wife was talking to the little girl. They were sitting next to each other in wicker chairs and my wife was asking her questions. She wanted to know how old she was and if she went to school. The little girl answered all her questions politely. She said *Yes, ma'am* and *No, ma'am* to all my wife's questions, but she didn't offer much beyond that. I could tell she was a very polite little girl, but also a little shy. I supposed it was the lip that did that. It might be hard to be outgoing with something like that. It would make you a little cautious, I would think.

My wife seemed to be really taken by the girl. She liked her. She didn't seem bothered at all by the deformed lip. I couldn't understand that. We were about to have a baby ourselves. It would at least have to enter your mind. There were so many things that could go wrong. That lip was just one of them. So far we'd made it through life without meeting up with any kind of real tragedy. We'd been making it through unscathed. But we knew it was out there. We knew it was out there around every corner. It might be just a matter of time before something happened to us.

I remembered hearing on the news about some Siamese twins that had recently been born. It was two little girls, joined at the hip and the chest and the head. The parents were considering having them separated. The doctors told them that often one of the babies will die. Sometimes both. How can you make a decision like that? I couldn't understand it. But the doctors were encouraging them to do it. They said it was the right thing to do.

The day was getting hot. The whole yard seemed to shimmer with heat. There were beads of sweat on my wife's face, some more running down her calves. Finally she said, "I can't take this anymore." She picked up her iced tea and moved into the shade of the back porch. Everyone else followed. Pretty soon we were all under the porch. It was still hot, but cooler than out in the sun. Dan fixed everyone fresh drinks then sat down and joined us under the porch.

We sat under the porch and talked. The little girl Anna was getting sleepy. She crawled into her mother's lap and put her head on her mother's shoulder. She didn't close her eyes, but they were getting heavy. Dan reached over to a table where there was a radio and turned it on. He turned it to a folk station, something he thought Anna would like. In a little while she closed her eyes. She started to breathe heavily. Her mother stroked her hair and hummed softly with the music. The rest of us watched Anna sleep. Her deformed lip didn't seem quite so monstrous and ugly when she slept. It was as if in sleep, relaxed as she was, it diminished a little.

My wife watched them with a warm smile on her face. She reached out and took my hand and put it in her lap. We watched Anna sleeping for a while and I left my hand in my wife's lap. Every once in a while I could feel the baby kick and my wife would give my hand a little squeeze. It was like she was saying, We're in this together. Just like Georgia and Anna. Soon we'll be just like them. Except there'll be three of us. We'll all be in it together. A family.

Then Steve said something about the lip. He couldn't keep his mouth shut. He wondered out loud if there wasn't a way to fix it. I was embarrassed. Embarrassed for Steve and for Georgia both, but it didn't seem to bother Georgia. She'd probably heard this kind of thing before. *Why haven't you done something about that? You're not going to let her go through life like that, are you?*

Georgia took a drink from her glass. There were beads of sweat all down the sides.

"There's a surgery that could fix it," she said. "But we haven't decided."

That should have been the end of it, but Steve couldn't stay quiet.

"Why not?" he asked. "Why can't you decide?"

Steve was wearing a dark shirt and there were sweat stains under his arms and down the front. He took an ice cube from his drink and held it on the back of his neck.

Georgia looked at him for a moment then looked out into the wavy heat of the yard.

"I don't know," she said. "It's who she is. It's a hard decision."

Steve slurped down the rest of his drink and set it on the cement between his feet.

"I'd do it," he said. "I'd want her to look normal."

My wife sat up a little. I could feel her muscles tighten.

"Who's to say what's normal?" she said.

Everyone else had had a few drinks. My wife had been drinking nothing but iced tea. I figured this gave her an advantage, a certain air of authority, but it didn't deter Steve.

"Normal," he said, "is like everyone else." He waved his hand at us. "Normal like us."

"Ignorant," said my wife.

"Why?" said Steve. "Why is that ignorant? What's your definition of normal?"

"Stop!" said Georgia. "I don't want to be the cause of this."

Nobody said anything for a while after that. It was an uncomfortable situation. My wife was not normally the kind to confront people, but she liked the little girl and I think she wanted to defend her. We were about to have a child of our own and that makes you think about things. She had a point, too. Who's to say what normal is? But the more I thought about it, although I hated to admit it, I thought Steve had a point, too. Normal is like us. Isn't that the way we think?

I didn't say anything. I didn't want to get into the mix. Pretty soon the song on the radio ended and the news came on. There was another report about the Siamese twins that had been born. We all listened. They were doing fine. They shared a couple of organs, but otherwise they were fine. They were ready to come home from the hospital. The parents were still considering the surgery, but they wanted to take them home and live with them for a while first. They wanted to show them where they were going to live. A doctor came on and said some words about the surgery, about what the procedure would be like. He said it was something that was better done sooner rather than later. I thought it sounded a little like he was bullying the parents. They weren't ready to decide. They wanted to take their twins home and get to know them a bit first.

We all listened. I left my hand where it was in my wife's lap. We were lucky. I knew that. We hadn't experienced anything that amounted to tragedy. Our parents were both still living. I had a good job and we had a nice house. We had friends to spend holidays with.

I must have fallen asleep for a while, because when I woke up the grill was going and Georgia had taken her girl inside and laid her on the couch. The sun was dipping down in the sky and somewhere in the neighborhood someone was setting off firecrackers. Steve was the only one left on the patio. He had his hat pulled down over his eyes and looked like he might be sleeping.

I looked at Dan standing by the grill with a pair of tongs in his hand. He'd put on an apron that looked like it was meant for a woman. The smoke came up from the grill and drifted across the yard. His wife came out of the house and put a bowl of potato salad on the table. My wife followed her holding a plate of deviled eggs and a bowl of chips. Everyone was making a valiant effort to resurrect the party, but I could tell it was a lost cause. Those Siamese twins had ruined it for us.

I went to the bathroom again and when I came out I didn't go back out to the backyard. Instead I walked into one of the bedrooms that faced the front of the house. It was one of Dan's boy's bedrooms. There were posters of sports figures on the walls and a shelf of trophies. There was a fish tank that gurgled bubbles.

I went to the window and looked out. Across the street a car pulled up and stopped. After a moment a woman emerged from the house and waved to the person in the car. It was probably her boyfriend, taking her somewhere to watch the fireworks. She jogged down the sidewalk and the person inside leaned over and opened the door. When she was inside, the car moved off down the street, and then turned a corner and went out of sight. I stood there for a long time watching the end of the street where it had disappeared. I was lucky, I knew that, but sometimes I wished someone would take me away like that, just drive me off into the distance.

I heard a noise and turned around. There was Georgia, lying on the bed. She'd come in for a nap, but now she was looking at me. I hadn't noticed she was there. I felt a deep empathy for her, for the kind of life she'd had, but I knew she wouldn't want my pity.

"I'm sorry for what Steve said," I said.

Georgia tilted her head and tucked some strands of hair behind her ear. There were some creases on her face from where it had rested on the pillow.

"It did bother me," she said. "I know I acted like it didn't. But it did."

I just stood there. I didn't know what to say. Georgia sat up in the bed, swinging her feet around to the floor.

"I liked what your wife said," she said. "About not knowing what normal is. The truth is I've always thought Anna wasn't normal. But I liked what your wife said. Who are we to say what it is? I think it's better to think like that. To realize that we don't really know."

Two weeks later my wife woke me up in the middle of the night by shaking my shoulder.

"I'm having contractions," she said.

"What?" I asked. "What did you say?"

"I'm in labor," she said.

I asked her how long she'd been having them and she said for several hours. She'd been lying awake for that long having contractions.

"Do you want to go to the hospital?" I asked.

"I think we should," said my wife.

The two of us got dressed and I threw some things into a bag for my wife. Her due date was several weeks off and we weren't prepared. We'd thought we had more time. When we got into the car I looked at my wife. I put my hand on her knee and asked her how she was feeling.

"I'm a little worried," she said. "It's early. This shouldn't be happening yet."

"I don't think it's anything to worry about," I said. "I think it's pretty common."

I didn't know if it was or not. I didn't know if there was something to worry about. All I knew was that it was best if she didn't worry, because that would only make things worse.

"Maybe it's false labor," I suggested.

My wife grimaced while another contraction hit. When it was over she managed a weak smile.

"I don't think so," she said. "I think this is the real thing."

I drove through the streets toward the hospital. It was the middle of the night and there were no other cars out. Every once in a while my wife would grip the armrest and clench her teeth. When it was over she would take deep breaths of air, like it was something she'd been deprived of for a long time.

At one point I made a wrong turn. I glanced at my

wife, but she hadn't noticed. She was busy with another contraction. I didn't say anything, because I didn't want her to worry. I just kept going the wrong way, hoping I could circle around and get back on track, but the farther I went the more lost I got. These were streets I didn't recognize, in a part of the city I'd never been in before. The streets were narrow and the buildings were tall and dark, hovering above us like giants.

My wife was between contractions so I asked her if she wanted me to turn on the radio, if hearing something would make things easier.

"Okay," she said. "Let's hear something."

I turned to a station that was playing some slow jazz and it did seem to help. My wife went through another contraction and the music seemed to help. She didn't clench her teeth so much and the breathing afterward was not as heavy. I thought the music was helping.

I was still lost, but I thought I was close to getting back on track.

Between contractions my wife looked out the window.

"Are we almost there?" she asked. "How are you taking us?"

"It's okay," I said. "We're almost there."

I didn't know if we were or not, but I knew it was important that she didn't worry. My wife started having another contraction and this time she moaned like someone was twisting her arm behind her back. I couldn't believe I'd gotten us lost. She was going to have the baby in the car and I wouldn't know what to do. I saw a street I thought I recognized and turned down it, but it was nowhere I'd ever been before.

After the contraction was over my wife panted and wiped at the sweat on her forehead. She looked out the window and put her face close to the glass.

"Where are we?" she asked. "How are you taking us?"

The next question she was going to ask was if we were lost, and I would have to admit that we were, that I'd gotten us lost while she was in labor and we were on the way to the hospital. But just then I turned down another street and I knew where we were. We were only a mile or so from the hospital.

"It's okay," I said. "We're going to make it. We're going to be fine."

The song on the radio ended and the news came on. We hadn't heard anything about the Siamese twins for a long time, but now there was a report. The parents had taken their babies home and settled in. They'd gotten the feel of being a family. They'd fed them and rocked them to sleep and changed the diaper that fit over both of them at once. They'd gotten the feel of it all.

The mother of the Siamese twins was being interviewed. They were back at the hospital, the same one we were on our way to, that's where the interview was taking place.

"We want them to have a normal life," the woman told the reporter. "It breaks our hearts to see them this way."

My wife looked at me. In the dim light of her eyes I

could tell she wasn't afraid for herself anymore.

Those parents. They had decided to have their babies separated.

FORDICIDIA

YEARS HAVE GONE BY and we are still in
love. Sometimes when we're feeling wistful and if the
kids are sleeping soundly, we walk out into the night and
make love in the springtime fields under a canopy of
pulsing stars. When we do, that first night of our love
comes back: the night we danced in the old farmer's
barn, the smell of the river rising up with the mist. I
remember how your body glistened like honey as we
swang through the hay dust. We danced and sang and
drank sweet wine from a jug that took two hands to hold
to our laughing lips. We had just met, but you showed

no awkward inhibitions. You had been reading the Greeks and had developed a Ceres complex. It was April. You told me that April was named after the Greek goddess Aphrodite, known to the Romans as Venus, the goddess of love and beauty. She was the daughter of Zeus and Dione. I wanted to worship you then, because to me you were love and beauty and your knowledge was depthless. You told me that Venus was known to the Phoenicians as Astarte and as Ashtoreth to the Hebrews and King Solomon, who built a temple to her. She was also called Cloacina by the Romans and Urania by the Greeks, and when I pointed out how confusing this might appear to be, you said, "Deal with it." And then you kissed me—our first—and your full lips tasted like wine and fruit and the springtime air.

But it was Ceres you fancied. When I asked about your parents you even went so far as to tell me their names were Saturn and Ops. You said you had a brother who'd sold his mustang and began commuting in a chariot. I loved you for that. You looked so beautiful in the dusty light of the barn, your cheekbones high and prominent, like they were chiseled from granite. In a moment of inspiration I told you you were fit for Ceres and that made you smile, because you said it was a common expression among the Romans and meant that something was splendid.

When the wine was gone and we had tired of dancing I thought we would go home, but you found a rusty axe and buried it deep between the shoulders of the farmer's Jersey cow. The cow didn't make a sound, only raised her head slightly to look at us, the blood percolating and bubbling in a dark deluge around her thick neck, and dropping like molasses onto the yellow hay and the worn floorboards. I remember how surprised we were when she didn't fall. You stood next to me then and took my hand and your thumping pulse soon fell into rhythm with mine. That cow, with the axe angling out of its back, was like a statue. After a time she closed her eyes, as if only sleeping, certainly not dead.

I was mystified, but you knew what to do.

I was struck by how well we fit together, how your shoulder and mine pressed against the cow's flank, your breasts on my back, our hips bumping with ribs, until at last she collapsed and the sudden silence of the barn was almost deafening.

I wanted to kiss you then. I wanted to suggest that we bathe in the river. But you mentioned Tellus, the earth goddess, and said there was work to do.

You knelt and ran your hands over the warm round flank of the cow and I was immediately aware, as you had been all along, of the calf we had awoken inside. I thought you were felicitous and excellent the way you located a hay knife and with surgical precision began slicing the leathery stomach with strokes that were laborious but also adept.

The first time I heard you swear it was at the farmer for keeping such a dull knife. You wiped the sweat from your face with the back of your hand, but you wouldn't let me help. I was only able to stand by like an acolyte as you performed your priestly duties. It was such a mild evening for April and as you worked a warm breeze blew through the barn and it carried with it the smell of things growing.

I was glad when we went outside. The night was dark and the stars throbbed like they had their own heartbeats. Your skin was glistening with sweat and the breeze made you shiver. When we built a fire using blackthorn and willow the golden light from the flames made your face and hair glow so radiantly that I thought that you might not be real. But then you put your hands around my neck and kissed me again, and this time I tasted grains—wheat and corn and hints of barley.

When we threw the calf onto the fire the gluttonous flames licked and hissed over its wet body, and soon there were billows of fleshy smoke rising like shadows into the earthy night.

As the fire burned we sat down nearby and discussed our future. I suggested marriage and was surprised at how easily you agreed.

"Where should we tie the knot?" you asked.

"Why not Baltimore?"

I don't know why I said it. It was a dumb thing to say and it clearly upset you. You wanted Constantinople or Rome, but when I pointed out the expense of such an endeavor you conceded that Athens, Georgia might suffice. It was a small setback in our relationship, but we quickly moved beyond it and began discussing children. This was a trickier issue because you'd once had a dream that you'd had a daughter and you'd lost her. After a long search you eventually found her again, but while she'd been lost she'd married a man who lived far away and now she only lived with you for six months out of the year. It was an arrangement, you said, that was not ideal, but which you could live with. In fact, you wanted children, scads of them.

Later in the night we gathered the ashes in a feed pail. You suggested we take off our clothes and we walked naked under the stars and threw handfuls of the warm ash into the air. I admired your body in the gauzy twilight, your hips and breasts so perfectly shaped, and the ash all around us as if we were wrapped in a cloud. It settled in our hair and on our shoulders and we could feel its sting in our nostrils and taste the bitter sharpness on our tongues. We walked through the sullen fields and down to the river that even in the uncertain light was so clear you could count the pebbles on the bottom. The willows shaded it, and the grassy bank sloped down to the water's edge. You approached and touched the water with your foot. Then you went in and beckoned me to follow. The water was warmer than I would have suspected and I wondered if the river at some point descended into deep caverns and was heated by the earth's fiery core. We stood for a while with the water lapping at our knees, but you were not content with that. Soon we were floating on our backs, the water coursing softly around us, the congregation of stars above and a few cooing doves our only audience.

We must have slept because I awoke with my arm pinned under your back, the soft morning sunlight making your angelic face look ethereal. We were lying in the middle of a field that had blossomed into a sea of wildflowers. There was foxglove and sweet william and bluebonnet and yarrow. You showed me a flower with backward projecting spurs and tightly compact blossoms arranged on spikes in shades of pink, white and deep blue, and told me it was rocket larkspur.

"This shouldn't even be here," you said.

There were wildflowers from all over the world, from Patagonia and Laos and Iceland. There was a delicate blue daisy that only grew in the Andes above 12,000 feet.

"What have we done?" I asked.

But we needn't have worried. The attention was soon on the farmer, who had always been famous for his unspectacular harvests. An extension agent came out from the university and measured his wheat, which was twice as tall as the neighboring farmer's. His corn was causing a stir in town. By June it was twelve feet tall and showed no sign of stopping. Once a carload of teenagers drove into it and didn't come out for two days. There was alcohol involved, but the local paper chose not to mention it. The reporter preferred to focus on the dangerous height of the corn, on liability issues, and even dared to suggest that perhaps something should be done about it.

But the farmer had other things on his mind. He was kept busy in the barn where his pigs were birthing record litters of sixteen and eighteen and once twenty-four. They were lively and robust piglets, with deep pink skin and never a runt among them. Of course there wasn't room for them all and soon they were seen cavorting in the grass around the farmhouse like puppies. They sometimes went for swims in the pond and had a special affection for digging up tulip bulbs.

At the café in town where we sometimes stopped for coffee the topic of conversation never varied. We would sit at the booth in the back and listen to the burgeoning gossip.

"He's doing something right."

"Or something illegal."

"I heard he was experimenting with genetic engineering."

"Or sold his soul to the devil."

"He always did keep to himself."

"I never did trust him."

"Leave the man alone."

By the end of the summer there was more fruit on his trees than his wife could possibly can, and anyway she was pregnant with twins. On Sunday afternoons you liked to walk through his orchard and then down to the river where the sun filtered through the willows and the grassy loam was soft under our heads. We would lie with our heads together and talk about the quiver-full of children we would have someday. But first you wanted to travel. You wanted to see the giant sequoias and the Badlands and the Serengeti. I told you I wouldn't be satisfied until I'd climbed El Capitan and swum the English Channel. I wanted to walk across Death Valley in August.

"Fine," you said. "But can we at least go to Colorado and see the elk?"

We watched the sunset and returned home. We were sleeping on a mattress on the floor at the time, because you couldn't stand to sleep so far away from the ground. Our house was full of potted plants—dwarf banana trees, and coffee plants and Santa Cruz cypress—things that no one else would think to grow. In the corner of our bedroom a startling shock of coyote thistle flourished. There was always dirt under your nails and you often smelled faintly of peat. I used to love to bury my face in your skin and inhale the fecundity. You were very tolerant, although I sensed at times you wished I'd just go into the other room and do some sit-ups. But we always fell asleep in each other's arms. You couldn't fall asleep unless you were touching me.

It was a hot summer, but there was often an overnight rain. In the mornings there was a sweet coolness and just a little humidity. I don't remember that we ever wore shoes. We would sit on our little front porch in the mornings drinking coffee and watching the robins gathering worms. Our topics of conversation invariably leaned to literature and recycling and alternative forms of energy. Our future seemed so radiant and bright then, like the farmer's endless fields of corn, stretching away to the horizon like a gold-tasseled sea.

When we weren't trespassing at the farmer's we were loitering in the park. We would go there to watch the children. We liked to play a little game where we pretended they were ours. We gave them names and imagined picking them up from school in the afternoon and helping them with their homework. We didn't mind the birthday parties and the diapers and the constant shuttling between soccer games and piano lessons. We were firm parents, emphasizing discipline and politeness and good hygiene, but never overly harsh. There were only a handful of children when we first started going, but after several weeks they began to multiply. Soon the place was overrun with the little cherubs.

"Look at all our children," you said.

What could I do but agree?

"Just look at them," I said.

One morning I found you at the kitchen table reading the paper. As I poured myself a cup of coffee you said, "Look here."

"What is it?"

"That farmer won seventeen blue ribbons at the county fair."

I realized it had been a long time since we'd been to the farmer's. We'd been spending so much time at the park watching the children that we'd neglected the farmer, so I suggested a picnic and you readily agreed.

But then for three days it rained and we were confined to the house. Luckily you had been stocking up on children's games in preparation for our own brood, so we had little time to be bored. We spent the whole day in our pajamas and played Candyland and Chutes and Ladders and Memory. You had an uncanny ability to win at Memory. We were surprised by how much we liked the games, especially Life, but at some point when you had a husband and a car full of kids and were adequately insured, you began to cry.

The next day you threw out all our detergents and cleaning supplies and then went on the Internet and learned how to make your own using vinegar and water and lemon juice. You gathered up the scissors and letter openers and put them in a basket on a high shelf. The curtain cords you cut off completely and burned them in the fireplace. You had me throw out all of our expired prescription drugs and put a lock on the medicine cabinet.

"So much to think about," you said.

I agreed that there was. I started to wonder if you were beginning to grow out of your Ceres complex. I hadn't seen you read any Greek mythology in weeks. But the next day the sun was shining and you were happy. You watered all the houseplants and put on a white blouse that I'd never seen before. It was a beautiful Indian summer day and by the time we got out to the farmer's it was almost hot. You produced a basket from the trunk of the car and I saw that it was stuffed with fresh bread and cheese and wine. On the way through the farmer's orchard we picked dozens of peaches. They were so sweet and juicy that we ate some of them as we walked. When we got to the river we washed our hands in the tepid water and sat down in the mottled shade under the willows. We talked for a while about baby names; you gravitated to the unusual, while I preferred the more traditional.

"Henry," I said.

"Zander," you replied.

"Elizabeth," I said.

"Aster," you said.

We both commented that the willow leaves were not as vibrant as they'd once been, that perhaps they were beginning to turn. Then a V of geese flew over and I could tell that it filled you with malaise. I suggested we eat more of the peaches and you dug in with abandon, the juice running in rivulets down your chin. You tossed the pits into the river and they sank and rolled along the pebbly bottom. Where would they end up? I wondered. In measureless caverns? At the bottom of a sunless sea?

In the distance we could see the farmer's wife. She came out of the farmhouse with a basket and began pinning clothes to a line. She was enormously pregnant. When she was done she picked up the basket, but paused for a moment and looked over the fields. We were too far away to see the features of her face but we imagined it was a face that in that moment was etched with both joy and melancholy, both hope and fear. You reached over and took my hand and then we watched as the farmer's wife brushed the hair away from her eyes and went inside. There was a sudden gust of wind and a few of the willow leaves drifted down around us.

"Soon winter," you said.

I didn't like to hear the deep despondency in your voice. It wasn't like you.

"Then spring," I said.

But you thought that was a habitual and clichéd thing to say.

"But true," I said.

"And inevitable," you said. "Like tornadoes and drought."

It was then I knew I had to get metaphorical with you, so I reminded you of that first night in the barn, how it had been the beginning of something the enormity of which we could never have fathomed. I reminded you that death gives birth to life and life descends into death and one can't exist without the other. I held up my hands, which were running with streams of fresh peach juice. I grabbed you by the wrists and pulled your own hands up in front of your face.

"And look," I said. "The blood is still fresh on our hands."

A GIRL & A CHAINSAW

I N   R E T R O S P E C T   we shouldn't have been working at all that day, but that morning I'd made the mistake of listening to the weather and had heard the forecast for rain. We'd been framing up a duplex on the south end of town and were only a day away from having it dried in. It was the Fourth of July weekend and most of my crew had already left for the lake, but I got a hold of Jimmy, ingenuous Jimmy, and told him I'd pay him time and a half.

I picked him up at a corner near his apartment and we were on the roof by seven. By nine we'd stripped off our shirts, but the heat was comfortable and we were used to it. In Montana the hottest part of the day doesn't come until late afternoon, and I thought we'd be done by then. I was already looking forward to it. I didn't have any plans for the weekend, only to sit out in the backyard under a sprinkler with a cooler of beer nearby, maybe catch a few innings of the All-Star game.

I was on the ground fetching something from my truck when Jimmy's nailer exploded. I turned around just in time to see him flipping off the edge of the roof, his foot catching for a moment on something at the eave. He landed on a pile of pit run, both hands still clasped to his face. The way he lay there, his back arched over the pile of gravel, I was sure it was broken, but when I got to him all he could talk about were his eyes.

"My eyes! My eyes!" he screamed. "They're on fire!"

There didn't seem to be anything wrong with his back, or anything else for that matter, which was miraculous after falling from a two-story duplex, but he kept screaming about his eyes and wouldn't take his hands away, so I couldn't get a look at them. When I got him into the truck he put his head back and stopped screaming, but still he didn't take away his hands. I got him to the hospital and they took him right in, and the whole time he never took his hands away from his face.

After he was gone, I didn't know what to do. No one had asked me anything. I didn't think it had even registered with anyone that I was the one who brought him in. It had all happened so fast. They whisked him away and I was left standing there wondering what to do. Was I supposed to wait? I had no idea how long he'd be gone. Should I leave and call in a couple hours to check in? I'd never done this kind of thing before, so I was lost. I walked over to a plate-glass window and stood in front of it. The light outside was harsh and the grass was a deep emerald green. A man on a riding lawn mower chugged over the lawn spitting the grass into a catcher behind him. I could hear the chugging of the lawn mower through the glass and there was something reassuring about that.

I stayed for a while then ended up going home. On the way I stopped by the job site and picked up the tools we'd left out. Jimmy's nail gun was still up on the roof, the piston busted through, the casing curled like a potato chip.

I went home and drank a beer on the couch then I called the hospital. The woman I talked to wanted to know what my relationship to the patient was and when I told her I was his boss she was satisfied, but she didn't have anything she could tell me. I hung up the phone and a few minutes later the doctor who had treated Jimmy called. He told me a lot of technical things I didn't understand—optic nerves and retinas—but essentially what he was saying was that Jimmy was going to be okay, only that he'd have to keep his eyes bandaged for a week or two. We worked it out that I'd pick him up the next morning. I told the doctor that Jimmy could stay at my place until the bandages came off, but he didn't seem concerned about that, only that I pick him up in the morning and get him out of there.

Later that evening I opened a beer and stepped outside. It was hot and the air was as still as something dead. Next door my neighbor's garage door was up and I heard her moving around in there. Sometimes there was a clanking sound like metal dropped onto cement. At the end of the driveway a few things, boxes and pieces of wood, were piled by the curb.

The neighbor's name was Nina. I didn't know her well, but I'd talked to her a few times over the years, taking out the trash or walking out to the mailbox. She was thin-boned and pretty, her hair light and straight, the color of champagne. She was originally from Oklahoma; I knew that much. She didn't ever wear makeup that I noticed, but then she didn't need to. She had that kind of natural beauty that the addition of makeup only detracts from. It was a quixotic beauty, tempered with a bit of sorrow. Her husband was a doctor, but I hadn't seen him, hadn't seen his car, in several weeks. I wondered if he'd left her, if this was why she was cleaning out her garage. I couldn't imagine wanting to leave a woman like that, but people do strange things.

I walked down to the end of the driveway with my beer. There was a fence between our two driveways, but it was less than waist high. On Nina's side there was a row of neatly spaced rosebushes. My side had grass, too long and full of dandelions. I crouched down and pulled a few then I heard Nina's voice. It was soft and a little husky, like maybe she'd been a smoker once, before she'd met the doctor, or maybe because she'd spent the last two weeks crying. She was standing at the edge of her driveway, right on the other side of the fence.

"Ken left me," she said.

I didn't know what to say, didn't know what my role was. I supposed moments like these brought neighbors together, but what was the protocol? All my life I'd felt like an outsider, like other people had more information, or more training, about how to act, what to say in certain situations. Susan knew this about me. It was, finally, what convinced her to leave. The last thing she said to me was, "You just don't get it." I didn't argue, because I couldn't. She was right. Lots of times I just didn't get it.

I looked at Nina from my crouching position.

"I hadn't seen his car in a while," I said.

Nina was looking at my beer. Her eyes were a pale green like olive oil.

"Do you want one?" I asked.

She ran a hand through her silky hair and said, "Okay."

I went back in and got her a beer, and when I came back out she was still standing in the driveway, just where I'd left her. She sipped at the beer like someone who hadn't had one very often. I guessed she was probably more of a wine drinker, but I didn't have wine. We stood there for a few moments with our beers and we made some small talk, about the weather, about the holiday weekend, the fireworks, then Nina looked at me as if she were sizing me up.

"You're about Ken's size," she said. "He left a bunch

of shirts. Do you want to take a look?"

I didn't want any of Ken's shirts, but I sensed that it was probably important to Nina, part of the cathartic process, so I told her I'd take a look. She led me into the house, through the living room, down the hall to the master bedroom, and opened the closet door.

"Take anything you want. I'm just going to take it to Goodwill."

The next morning I brought Jimmy home from the hospital. He had patches over his eyes and gauze wrapped around his head. He was looking like a casualty off a battlefield, but he was feeling much better. They'd put something in his eyes that had stopped the burning. Jimmy sat erect in the seat next to me, his elbow hanging out the open window. He turned his head left and right, as if he were trying to see.

Halfway home I stopped at a red light and several people crossed on the crosswalk in front of us. Among them was a man whose torso and arms and neck were covered in tattoos. He had taken off his shirt and was carrying it balled up in his hand. I must have let out a low whistle, because Jimmy said, "What?"

"Nothing," I said. "There's just a guy with tattoos. Lots of them."

Jimmy wanted to know what the tattoos looked like, but there were so many, so densely packed together, that it was hard to distinguish one from another. But I felt sorry for Jimmy with his eyes bandaged, living in that darkness, so I told him there were birds—eagles and owls and hawks and ravens, and across his back, covering almost all of it, a phoenix with fiery red eyes rising from a pool of ashes.

"Wow," said Jimmy. "I wish I could see that."

At the house I got him settled on the couch and gave him a cup of coffee. Jimmy seemed to need to be oriented a bit, so I walked around the living room touching tables and chairs and lamps, and described things, letting him follow the sound of my voice. I'll admit I embellished a little, but it was only so that he would feel comfortable, so that he would feel that he was in a nice place.

Later in the morning Jimmy took a nap and I went back to the duplex to finish up the roof. There were dark clouds coming in from the west and it looked like the promised rain was on its way, but I was able to get the roof finished up before anything happened. I was just getting home when the first drops started to fall.

Nina was still working on the garage, and the pile at the curb had grown. Among the trash I spotted a bright orange chainsaw case. It just happened that I needed a chainsaw case. Susan had bought me a chainsaw for my last birthday, but it hadn't come with a case. I walked over to the pile and Nina saw me and waved from the garage, so I pointed to the case.

"Are you throwing this away?"

Nina took a few steps out of the garage and nodded, the large drops of rain speckling the shoulders of her white shirt like age spots.

"It was Ken's," she said.

I stood there for a moment, sorry that I'd been the cause of her using his name. She looked small and frail framed the way she was in the large garage door, but there was also a sinewy toughness about her, something that spoke of resilience.

"Do you mind if I take it?"

Nina approached and we stood for a moment in the warm rain. We looked together down at the orange case, like it might contain something that required something, something like energy or emotion.

"Not at all," said Nina. "Go right ahead."

I picked up the case and discovered immediately that it did contain something. I glanced at Nina, whose hair was darkened by the rain, and opened the case. There inside was a bright red chainsaw, complete with owner's manual and a wrench/screwdriver. I didn't know what to do except state the obvious.

"There's a saw in here," I said.

"Yeah," said Nina. "Ken could never get it to start. He said the rope handle thing wouldn't pull."

I gripped the saw with one hand and pulled the cord with the other and, sure enough, it didn't budge.

"I see what you mean," I said.

"Yeah," said Nina.

I didn't know what else to say. The rain was becoming steadier, the drops smaller.

"I can't take this," I said at last. "It's brand new."

"Oh please," said Nina. "You'd be doing me a favor."

She walked away, back into the garage, and I

watched until her tiny frame disappeared into the darkness.

Inside, I set the chainsaw down in the entryway. Jimmy was awake, still sitting on the couch.

"What's that?" he asked.

"A chainsaw," I said. "The neighbor gave it to me, but it doesn't work."

"I heard you talking out there," said Jimmy. "She sounded nice."

"Her husband left her."

"That's too bad," said Jimmy. "Is she pretty? She sounded pretty."

"Not really," I said. "She may have been once. Not any more. She's let herself go. She doesn't take care of herself."

"That's too bad," said Jimmy. "She sounded pretty."

"She has a proportion problem," I said. "Her head's too large for her body."

"And her arms are too short," said Jimmy. "Like a dwarf or a midget."

"That's right," I said.

"I can see it," said Jimmy. "I've seen people like that before."

I stood at the doorway to the kitchen feeling the rain water slipping out of my hair and running down the back of my neck. The windows were all open and there was a thick humidity to the room, but the rain outside had stopped.

"What do you say we throw some big steaks on the grill," I suggested.

Jimmy smiled.

"Big as Rottweilers," he said.

"Big as Rottweilers," I agreed.

The clouds moved through and we cooked up the steaks. When we were done eating we sat on the back deck and enjoyed the coolness. Behind my house and Nina's, down a sloping hill and surrounded by short pines, was a small duck pond. It was really nothing more than a swamp, reedy and murky, but the ducks liked it. Jimmy heard a quack and a violent flapping of wings and asked me what it was.

"A couple of coots," I said. "Probably fighting over a piece of algae."

"What do they look like?" asked Jimmy.

Coots are pretty plain; just black feathers and a tiny head with a white beak. I thought Jimmy would be disappointed, so I threw in some color.

"They're slate-black," I said. "Their beaks are yellow and they have a red crown on their heads. Their eyes are either orange or gold, depending on the light."

"What color are they now?" asked Jimmy.

"Right now they're gold," I said. "Like the sun on the horizon."

"What else?" asked Jimmy.

He reached into the cooler and came up with a can of beer. He'd already had several and I noticed he'd started to slur. There was nothing else on the pond, but a week earlier I'd seen some grebes and a pair of mergansers.

"There's grebes and mergansers," I said. "A little while ago there were some goldeneyes, but they're gone now."

"What are they like?" asked Jimmy.

"Dark, round heads, brilliant white sides, a brown stripe down the middle of their backs."

"Are they beautiful?" asked Jimmy.

"Yeah, beautiful," I said. "Like nothing you've ever seen."

The next morning I found Jimmy sitting on the back deck in one of my bathrobes. I handed him a cup of coffee and sat down next to him.

"What's that smell," he asked.

I wasn't sure what he was smelling, but I took a stab.

"It's the pine trees," I said. "In the morning they open up their cones and this smell comes out. It's like honey and sap, and Chinese five spice."

Jimmy thought for a moment and breathed, satisfied with my answer.

"It's going to be nice today, isn't it."

"Yeah," I said. "It's the Fourth of July. It's going to be hot, but there won't be any humidity. It's going to be that kind of heat that you can feel down in your bones, like magma bubbling up from your insides."

"Yeah," said Jimmy. "I can feel that."

We sat for a while and felt the heat of the day already beginning to rise up. Jimmy finished his coffee and cradled the cup in his lap.

"Maybe later we can have a look at that saw," he said.

"Okay," I said. "We'll take a look at it later."

*   *   *

I decided to mow the lawn, not so much because I felt like mowing it, but because I was hoping to run into Nina, but she seemed to be finished with the garage. Her house was dark and quiet, and the garage door was down. When I finished with the lawn I went inside and found Jimmy sitting in the entryway with the chainsaw on his lap. He was just holding it, nothing else, like he thought a little tenderness might cure whatever was wrong. I sat down next to him on the cool tile.

"What do you think?" I asked.

"It's brand new," he said.

"Brand new," I said.

"Is there an owner's manual?" he asked.

I pulled the case over and lifted out the owner's manual. On the fourth page I found a little box that said, "Attention: During transit, oil from the automatic chain oiler can seep into the cylinder, creating a condition called 'hydraulic lock.' This will prevent the operator from being able to pull the starter cord. To correct this condition, remove the spark plug, pull the starter cord several times to dispel the excess oil, replace the spark plug and follow the normal starting procedure."

I read it out loud for Jimmy and he said, "Well, well, well."

I grabbed the wrench from the case and removed the spark plug. When I pulled the starter cord a bit of oil seeped out. Then I replaced the spark plug and tugged on the cord and the saw started on the very first pull. It ran like a brand-new saw, because it was. There I was standing in my house with a running chainsaw. I revved it a few times and the living room filled with blue smoke. Jimmy was laughing and clapping his hands, like I'd performed some kind of magical feat. Then I realized that the whole neighborhood could probably hear the saw and I quickly turned it off. Jimmy stopped laughing and grew serious. After a long moment he said, "Man, you gotta give her back that saw."

I knew I did, but I didn't want to. Not because I wanted to keep it, but because I knew she didn't want it, because I knew what it meant for her. Still, it had to go back.

That evening I propped a ladder against the side of the house and Jimmy and I crawled up to the shed dormer on the back of the roof. I ascended the ladder right behind him, making sure he took his time and didn't miss a rung. When we were halfway up Nina called to us from her backyard.

"Hey," she said. "What are you doing?"

I looked over my shoulder at her little silhouette in the fading light. She was wearing capri pants and a light teal camisole. She was barefoot and holding a glass of wine. I imagined for a moment what it would be like to hold her, to engulf her with my arms, to encase her until she practically disappeared.

"The fireworks," I said. "You can see them from the roof."

Nina tilted her head a little and brushed away a strand of hair that had caught at the corner of her mouth.

"Can I come?" she asked.

She went back inside and reemerged with a backpack over her shoulder. As she climbed the ladder the bottles she'd put in it clanked against each other like chimes. When she got to the eave of the dormer I took her hand, which was moist and small and nearly lost in my own. I introduced her to Jimmy and told her how he'd hurt his eyes. Then the three of us settled down, Nina between Jimmy and me, and leaned our backs against the steeper pitch of the roof.

Nina put the backpack between her legs and pulled out several dusty bottles of wine.

"We have a 1985 Cabernet from Sonoma," she said for Jimmy's benefit. "And a 1989 claret from France. And for dessert, a 1996 Grahams port."

"You didn't get those at Safeway," I said.

"Ken fancied himself a wine collector," she said.

She produced a corkscrew and opened one of the bottles then pulled out some plastic cups and poured us all some wine. I wasn't sure what I should do. I wasn't much of a wine drinker and this was good wine. Should I sniff? Swirl? Let it breathe a while before taking a sip? But Jimmy dug right in and so did Nina, so I took a sip too. I was expecting someone to say something, about how the wine tasted, using descriptors like cinnamon and blackberry and twigs, but no one did. We just sat and drank in the descending darkness until something moved at the edge of the pond and Jimmy asked what it was.

It was just Nina's cat, a little calicoed thing, but the

wine was so good, the night so warm and enveloping that I couldn't help myself.

"It's a bobcat," I said. "He's at the edge of the water tearing at a rabbit, or maybe it's a muskrat. He's ripping it to pieces. He has teeth like on a Skilsaw."

Jimmy took a sip of wine and whistled.

"Man, that cat's teeth are sharp," he said.

I looked at Nina, but she was gazing down at the pond where the cat was sitting quietly at the water's edge. Her eyes narrowed in the darkness, but she wasn't thinking about the cat, or the bobcat, not even Ken, but something else. She was a good companion, and Jimmy and I were lucky to have found her. She had her own tale of woe, like we all did, but she didn't feel compelled to tell it. She wasn't looking for sympathy, only the closeness of another human. It was enough to know that in a world of billions of people you weren't entirely alone.

A half moon began to rise above the far-off mountains and Jimmy must have sensed the change in the light.

"Is there a moon?" he asked.

I looked at Nina, her face muted in the soft moonlight, and she smiled her sorrowful smile.

"Yes," I said. "It's half full. It's making the trees look like they're gilded in gold leaf."

"Oh, and look," said Nina. "Now you can see the turkeys."

"Turkeys?" said Jimmy.

"Wild turkeys," said Nina. "There's a dozen or so of

them. In the trees by the pond. They must have gone up there to escape the bobcat."

I looked at her, small as a child, her face turned up to the moonlight.

"And some deer," I said. "They just wandered out of the woods. They're having a drink on the far side of the pond."

"Beautiful," said Nina. "The way the moonlight shines off their coats."

"Yeah, beautiful," said Jimmy. "I can see it."

He finished his wine and Nina took the bottle, and refilled all our glasses. It was fully dark now, except for the moonlight, and I thought the fireworks would be starting any time.

Nina leaned forward, into the night, and closed her eyes.

"Oh," she said. "Was that an owl that just flew over?"

"Was it?" asked Jimmy.

"I think it was," I said. "Enormous."

Just then the first of the fireworks erupted; a burst of blue and gold and green, opening up in the sky like a flower. Nina and I took turns describing them to Jimmy. We used words like heart-shaped and supervermilion and bloodburnt and uranium rays. And then there was an explosion of light that seemed like it was right above us and Nina told Jimmy it was like rosy flames flapping out of vents, and I wanted to kiss her for that. The next one erupted and I said it was the hot pink gills flaring on a tropical fish. Nina said a gold splash in your heart then coming out of your eyes and I said like a fume of smoke curves around a cupid fountain spurting fire.

Then right before the finale there was a pause, and during that pause we heard the hooting of an owl, far off and mournful.

"There's that owl," said Jimmy.

Then nobody said anything. Maybe we were all thinking the same thing: That there is a tremendous amount of goodness in the world, but that it's found in the numerous little things, that perhaps happiness is not to be found in the big passions, but in the small moments when no one seems to be noticing.

There was another eruption of light, the big finale. They came one on top of the other and filled the entire night sky.

I said, "Metallic sepia lipstick smeared on a pretty girl's mouth and bee wings stuck on her cheeks."

And then I felt Nina's tiny little hand touching mine, her fingers cupping into my palm, and she said, "A drop of moisture glistening on the middle of your upper lip."

And I knew then that I wouldn't have to return the saw. That it was mine to keep.

TOOL SALE

A TESTAMENT to Benjamin's relationship with his father: His father has worked for Bank of America all his life, and yet Benjamin couldn't say exactly what he did. It wasn't called Bank of America when his father started there in his early twenties. Benjamin doesn't know what they called it then, but Bank of America is what they call it now. It's the name, until recently, that was printed in red and blue ink on his father's pay checks. His father's job had something to do with acquisitions and mergers. He traveled a lot, mostly to other countries, countries where the systems of government were often younger than Benjamin. On the rare evenings when his father was home he sat in a wing-backed chair, a glass of amber liquid at his elbow, his face buried in financial reports printed on perforated paper. He was a person Benjamin had known, and yet not known, his entire life.

When his father retired, Benjamin allowed himself a moment of guarded expectation. When his father converted his garage into a woodworking shop and started outfitting it, the hesitation began to flake away. Soon he was calling Benjamin on the telephone, something in the past that only his mother had done. Sometimes he called two or three times a week asking for advice about tools—brands, horsepower, size requirements, accessories, whether to go 110 or 220. His shop wasn't large, but he made economical use of the space he had. His table saw was on wheels, tucked into a corner. When he needed it, he'd wheel it into the center of the room, rip his boards, then wheel it back, immediately shop-vacing the sawdust he'd created. His shop was always impeccably neat—a constant admonishment of Benjamin's.

Benjamin's father had a colleague he'd known for years who'd died of a stroke on the way home from his retirement party. When the paramedics arrived they found his wife kneeling beside him on the shoulder of the highway giving him mouth-to-mouth while traffic hissed by on the wet macadam. When the paramedics took over, the wife went to the car and retrieved the gold watch the company had given him. She shook it violently in her husband's face until one of the paramedics pulled her away and gave her a sedative. Benjamin's father has told him this story more than once. It's clear his father thinks there's a lesson there to be learned, but it's unclear to Benjamin if his father is comfortable with what it is.

Benjamin thought his father was dealing with retirement a little like a stroke victim who needs to relearn how to walk and talk. In that sense, Benjamin saw the woodworking as good therapy. Within two months his father had outfitted a shop that Benjamin was secretly envious of. But besides the envy, Benjamin also had to wonder if his father wasn't over-extending himself. He wondered if his mother, who for years had been talking about a trip to Norway when they retired, had an opinion about it. Benjamin wondered if their retirement savings could withstand outfitting the shop and still support the trip to Norway.

Benjamin's mother was the kind of woman who would only assert her opinion on topics she felt to be within her realm of expertise. Traditional borders prevailed. The kitchen and laundry room were hers; she had a sewing room in the basement, but she had no jurisdiction over the shop.

To balance Benjamin's envy, however, was the feeling that he now had a comrade in arms, someone he could use as a foil when his own wife accused him of buying tools he didn't need.

Like the time Benjamin had gone to the hardware store for a closet rod and come home with a biscuit jointer. Whenever Benjamin comes home with a new tool Beth wants to know what it's for, how much it cost, why it's so necessary, why one of his other tools couldn't accomplish the same thing. Beth doesn't understand the difference between a radial arm saw and a compound miter saw and, to be honest, it's hard for Benjamin to explain, but he usually manages by reverting to the elusive woodworking vocabulary that he's starting to share with his father. He talks about mortises and tenons and dadoes and rabbits and dovetails. It sounds impressive and has the desired effect of making Beth feel out of her realm.

Benjamin's other strategy, and one that usually works to a degree, is to explain to Beth that, although the tools are expensive, in the long run they're actually saving money.

"Remember when I put a new roof on the garage last year? We saved enough on just that one job to justify the nailer."

But the biscuit jointer is more difficult to explain. He doesn't even have a specific project in mind when he buys it. He doesn't really know why he's bought it, except that the black and yellow casing has stirred something deep inside him and he likes the way the words biscuit jointer sound when they roll off his tongue. On the way home from the hardware store he repeats it aloud several times *biscuit jointer, biscuit jointer, biscuit jointer,* and the sound of it within the protected dome of the car makes his heart swell.

He and Beth stand in the kitchen facing each other with the island between them while Benjamin tries to explain just what a biscuit jointer is for and why he needs one. In the end Beth levels a blow that Benjamin feels is below the belt.

"It's okay to own some tools, Ben. Just make sure they don't end up owning you."

Week by week his father's shop has been filling up—a drill press, a router, a 12-inch planer, bits and blades and jigs and vices. Now, the only thing the shop lacks is a jointer, so when Benjamin hears about the tool sale, he calls his father.

A week earlier on the Fourth of July he and Beth were down at his parents' house on the lake for a barbecue and to watch the fireworks that were launched from a platform in the middle of the bay.

"I think I need a jointer," said his father as he rotated ears of corn on the grill. "I think that's the last thing I need."

Benjamin looked in through the kitchen window where Beth and his mother were slicing fruit for a salad. After flipping the corn, his father closed the lid of the grill and glanced at his watch then looked out over the lake where a speedboat was racing along pulling a woman on skis. Benjamin stood next to his father and watched as the boat turned sharply and the woman swung outside the wake hitting waves from another boat. She almost fell, but then miraculously recovered.

"Wow," said his father.

Benjamin could feel the distance between the two of them, but it was a chasm that was narrowing. Before his father's retirement Benjamin would never have stood on the deck alone with his father for this long; the silence would have been palpable. But with the advent of the woodworking there has been a new sphere in which to exist with his father, and Benjamin is afraid it won't last.

Benjamin hears about the tool sale from his friend Martin who is a real estate agent. Martin has a new client, a man named Phil Campbell, who is liquidating everything—his house, his cars, his guns, his shop.

"This guy's shop is out of the skull crazy with tools," says Martin. "And most of it's hardly been used."

After the biscuit jointer Benjamin knows he shouldn't be buying any new tools for a while, but he thinks of his father.

"Does he have a jointer?" asks Benjamin.

"I think so," says Martin. "I'm pretty sure I remember him mentioning a jointer. Besides it would be insane if he didn't. I'm telling you he's got everything. Some of it in triplicate."

On the night before the tool sale, Beth and Benjamin make love, then lie side by side on top of the covers and let the air from a floor fan cool them. It's turned hot and Benjamin wonders what effect this will have on the tool sale. Do people buy more tools when it's hot, or fewer? Although he's not planning on buying anything, he wants to get there early, before things get picked over. He's told his father that he'll pick him up at six-thirty. Benjamin calculates that that should get them to the tool sale by seven-thirty. Not rudely early, but not too late either. He wants his father to have a shot at that jointer. He feels personally obligated to make it happen.

When Beth reaches over and touches his hand, Benjamin suddenly feels grateful. He knows that marriage is a living, malleable thing, that it ebbs and flows like a tide, that at times a husband and wife can be as if from one rootstock and at others can be like satellites that have lost their orbit.

They are nearing the end of their seventh year of marriage, the year when they've been told many couples have trouble, lose the energy for the work that marriage requires. But Benjamin and Beth have.made it through the seventh year and, if anything, their marriage is better than ever. They still laugh at each other's jokes. They can still cheer each other up when one of them is down. They still sometimes surprise each other with a little gift when no occasion calls for it. They still make love regularly.

Benjamin remembers a time when his family still lived in the East, when he was a child, perhaps five years old, when he got lost at a department store. He was with his sister and mother. There must have been a big sale, because the store was crowded. His mother had been holding his hand, when suddenly she let go and he was lost in a crowd that enveloped him like a cloak. He remembered from kindergarten that what you were to do if ever you got lost was stay put, don't move, so he stood motionless right where he was and wept silently as a throng of people jostled around him. Then there was a giant of a black man kneeling in front of him telling him not to cry. The black man took Benjamin's hand and led him out of the crowd and told him in the deepest voice that Benjamin had ever heard that he would help him find his mother.

Benjamin stopped crying. He felt safe with the black man, with the way the black man's hand swallowed up his own, with the way he held it firm, but not too tight. They walked around the store for hours and Benjamin marveled at the man's patience. Didn't he have anywhere he needed to be? The man asked him if he liked baseball, if he liked the Orioles' chances that year, if he ever got to go to the games. Benjamin marveled still more when he realized at some point that he didn't really want to find his mother, at least not yet. He wanted the black man's voice to go on and on, for it to be the last thing he heard before he fell asleep at night.

At last they found his mother and the black man released Benjamin's hand.

"He was lost and I found him," he said. "He was scared so I talked to him about baseball."

Just before getting married to Beth, something reminded Benjamin of that day in the department store and he asked his mother if she remembered it, too.

"Of course, I remember," she said. "You don't lose your baby, even if it's for only a few minutes and don't remember."

"A few minutes?" said Benjamin. "I was gone for hours."

"Honey, it wasn't anything like hours. It couldn't have been more than a minute or two. I barely knew you were gone before I found you."

"But what about the black man?" asked Benjamin.

"Black man?" said his mother. "There was no black man. I found you myself. You were only about twenty feet away standing behind a sock tree."

Sometimes when Beth touches him, that day in the department store comes back. He feels again that comfort, that firm warmth, the feeling that he's safe.

Benjamin and his father drive for an hour, mostly in silence, sipping slowly at the coffee that Benjamin's mother has provided for them in matching travel mugs. The tool sale is on the outskirts of a neighboring town. It's a smaller town than theirs, poorer, more blue collar. There's an aluminum plant that used to run four shifts, twenty-four hours a day until it shut down and put half the town out of work. That was several years ago. Now there's once again smoke rising from the plant's huge stack, but they're only running two shifts, and there are always rumors that they will shut down again.

The morning air is still cool when Benjamin and his father turn down a long gravel lane lined with aspen trees. They pull up in front of a large, aluminum-sided shop just as someone inside lifts open the expansive overhead door. There's a cardboard sign hanging to the side of the door: EVERYTHING FOR SALE.

There's a faint buzzing like electricity inside Benjamin's head, which could be the coffee, but more likely is something sparked by the realization that they are the first ones there.

Benjamin and his father sit still for a moment, then place their travel mugs on the dash in unison.

"That must be Phil," says Benjamin.

"Let's see what he's got," says his father.

Benjamin guesses that Phil is about his own age, or maybe a few years older. He could be forty, maybe forty-five. His longish wavy hair has begun to turn gray and his belly protrudes in front of him stretching out his blue T-shirt like a balloon. Martin has warned Benjamin that Phil is a talker, but he's unprepared for how forthright he is. As Phil shows them around the shop, Benjamin and his father ask only about the tools, but Phil continually offers personal information, so much that it's embarrassing. Without asking, they learn what they never wanted to know: the reason for the sale.

Phil's wife is sick. There's something wrong with her muscles, or with the way her brain communicates with her muscles. There are good days and not so good days, but lately the good days are harder to come by.

Phil holds up a box with a picture of a cutout tool on it.

"Never been out of the box," says Phil. "But I understand it's a very useful tool."

Martin had not been exaggerating when he told Benjamin about Phil's shop. There are more tools here than Benjamin has ever seen in his life and most of them look as if they've hardly been used.

Phil stoops down and picks up a chainsaw that has

the words "Farm Boss" written across the bar in orange letters.

"Need a chainsaw?" he asks. "I've only used it once. Everything's got to go."

Phil tells them there is an experimental surgery that could make his wife better, but that the insurance company won't pay for it.

"It's a shame," he says. "I haven't even had a chance to use some of this stuff. Now it's all got to go."

Phil stops before a bench grinder and listlessly turns it on. As it whirs up to speed he glances around the shop indifferently. When he turns back to the grinder he seems a little surprised to find it running. He smiles weakly at Benjamin and his father and turns it off.

"I'll sell you everything for fifteen thousand dollars," he says. "That's a bargain. It's worth twice that."

Benjamin looks outside and sees that two pickup trucks have pulled up and their occupants are climbing out.

"What about a jointer?" says Benjamin. "My father needs a jointer."

"Sure," says Phil.

There's a twinge of disappointment in his voice, as if he'd actually thought that someone might come in and buy everything at once, that he could be rid of it all that easily.

As Phil leads them to the jointer, Benjamin sees a woman enter the shop carrying several pieces of mail. She walks intentionally, carefully, but even so she can't hide the slight drag of her left foot, the toes not wanting to lift up, to point forward the way she wants them to. Benjamin flushes when he looks at her face, a face he knew once, a lifetime ago, before it began to sag at the cheeks, as if the muscles there now refuse to do their job, to keep that flesh high and proud on those once pronounced cheekbones.

It takes him a minute to remember her name. At first all he can think is that it begins with a K. There was a time in his life when he dated a string of women whose names began with K. Kendy, Kristin, Kirsten, Karen, Kay. But this is none of those. This is Kathy.

Benjamin watches her approach and waits for the recognition. She stands next to Phil, who is talking about the jointer, but when he notices her he stops in mid-sentence, then quickly, with unbridled pride, introduces her to Benjamin and his father.

She shakes their hands, then says, "Oh. Benjamin."

After a quick explanation of how they know one another, *We dated about a thousand years ago,* Kathy says she was just going to walk to the mailbox at the end of the lane and why doesn't Benjamin join her.

"It'll give us a chance to catch up," she says.

"Are you sure you're up to that?" asks Phil.

"Yes," says Kathy. "I think I'm going to have a good day."

Phil leans down and kisses her on the temple.

"Don't overdo it," he says.

Kathy and Benjamin walk down the gravel lane flanked by aspen trees quaking in the breeze. The day is beginning to heat up and Benjamin thinks that when he drops his father off back at his house he will take a dip in the lake before heading home to Beth.

"So," says Kathy.

She seems to be walking better now, with less effort, and the droop in her cheeks seems to have lessened.

"You're married," she says.

"Yes," says Benjamin. "Seven years. Her name is Beth."

Hearing Beth's name come out of his mouth it suddenly occurs to Benjamin that maybe all along, through all those years of dating, he was perhaps just looking for a woman whose name didn't begin with the letter K. He has had friends who agonized over marriage, who dated the same person for years before finally tying the knot. Not so with Benjamin and Beth. They knew after six months that they would get married. It wasn't really even a decision, but rather the natural next step in their relationship. Benjamin and Beth don't even have a good proposal story. Benjamin never actually proposed. They were lying in bed one night talking and somehow the subject of marriage came up.

"Do you think we should get married?" asked Benjamin.

"I do," said Beth.

Benjamin remembers driving into town the next day and thinking, *Wow, I'm engaged. How did that happen?* It felt like something that had simply happened to him in the natural course of things, not a decision he had made for himself. But rather than scaring him, this thought gave him comfort. That's the way it should be, he thought.

Now, as Benjamin walks with Kathy and listens to her talk about where her life has taken her since they last met—winery tour guide, tree trimmer at a Christmas tree farm, special ed aide at a rural school—it occurs to him how easily it could have turned out differently. How just as easily he could have been one of those other kind of couples.

"When did we break up?" asks Benjamin.

Kathy laughs.

"Don't you remember?" she asks.

"I'm sorry," he says. "I don't."

"We never did," says Kathy. "Officially, we're still dating."

Kathy looks at Benjamin, but he stares at her blankly.

"You went off to New Zealand for a year," she says. "Then when you got back you went off to grad school in Colorado. According to the rules of etiquette, we're still a couple."

Kathy's left foot suddenly refuses to do what it's supposed to. The toe of her shoe catches on a rock and she stumbles forward, but Benjamin catches her by the arm before she falls.

"Thank you," she says after she's recovered. "It's frustrating when your body stops listening to you."

"I can't even imagine," he says.

As they continue to walk, Benjamin lingers closer to Kathy's elbow in case she stumbles again. He looks at the mailbox, still a hundred yards distant, and wonders if she'll be able to make it. She is visibly concentrating now, willing her foot and ankle to flex and rise and move. A little glistening of sweat is forming at her temples.

"Am I hearing that you need closure?" asks Benjamin.

"Closure is always nice," says Kathy.

"We're through," says Benjamin. "I don't think we should see each other any more. I want to see other people. This isn't working out."

"There. Was that so hard? Don't you feel better? Now we can both get on with the rest of our lives."

"I do feel better," says Benjamin. "When I tell my wife tonight that I ran into you, it will go much better if I don't have to refer to you as my girlfriend."

On the way back, they stop a hundred or so yards from the shop. Phil and Ben's father are struggling to load the jointer onto the truck, both of them beginning to break into a sweat.

"Your husband must be sad to see all this go," says Benjamin. "I've never seen such a nice shop."

"He doesn't know it yet, but he'll be glad when it's all gone," says Kathy. "He's been trying to convince himself for years that he's a woodworking kind of guy, but he doesn't even enjoy it. He likes to buy tools, but he hates to use them."

"I'm glad I ran into you today," says Benjamin.

Kathy smiles at Benjamin, but the smile is only half there, the flesh on one side of her face drooping with fatigue, as if the muscles have separated, like cooked meat pulling away from a bone.

* * *

After unloading the jointer into the shop, Benjamin and his father are both hot and sticky with sweat. They put on bathing suits and dive into the lake. The water is cold and at first takes Benjamin's breath away, but after a minute it simply feels perfect. They swim for a while, then Benjamin drives home to Beth.

The house is empty when he arrives, but after getting himself a beer from the refrigerator, he sees Beth in the backyard, on her hands and knees, weeding their small vegetable garden. She's wearing blue shorts and a white tank top with little blue flowers on it. Her long brown hair is tied back in a ponytail, in a way that makes her seem girlish, almost like a teenager. He notices how sinewy and muscular her arms and shoulders are, how tanned and smooth. When she sits up for a moment and wipes her forehead with the back of her hand, he sees a little rippling of muscle move across her back. He gets another beer from the refrigerator and goes out and sits near her on the grass.

Beth looks at the beer he hands her and smiles.

"Is it noon, yet?" she asks.

"It is somewhere," he says.

Beth sits and sips her beer and they look at the garden together.

"Well," she says. "Tell me about this magnificent tool sale."

"It was amazing," says Benjamin. "I've never seen a shop like this. This guy had everything two or three times over and most of it had hardly been used. He kept holding things up for us to see and saying things like,

'I've only used this once or twice.' It was all top-of-the-line, too."

"Did your father get his jointer?" asks Beth.

"Yeah," says Benjamin. "He got it."

They both sip their beers and watch as a pair of bright blue butterflies enter the garden and begin weaving in and out of the vegetables. When the butterflies move on to the neighbor's yard, Benjamin reaches over and touches the nape of Beth's neck. The skin is hot, moist with perspiration, but also smooth and taut like a piece of rope.

"And what about you?" asks Beth. "What tool or tools were there that you couldn't live without?"

Benjamin finishes his beer and rolls the empty bottle between his palms.

"I guess there was nothing there I couldn't live without," he says.

"You didn't get anything?" asks Beth.

There is genuine surprise in her voice.

"Not a thing," says Benjamin.

Beth looks at him for a minute, as if trying to decipher some kind of code.

"Do you know why I love you?" she asks.

"Tell me," says Benjamin.

"Because just when I think I've got you figured out, you do something that surprises me."

"If I were consistent you might get bored," says Benjamin.

That night in bed they begin the motions of lovemaking,

then decide that it's too hot and give up. As they lie side by side on top of the covers, the floor fan quietly whirring in the corner, Benjamin feels a restlessness growing inside him. He wants to tell Beth more about the tool sale. He wants to explain to her that it was more than just tools, more even than the reason that they had to be sold. He wants to tell her about how he felt as they were leaving, as a dozen or more cars and trucks were streaming in as they were going out.

Benjamin lies in bed with his eyes closed and imagines Phil standing in the middle of his shop as it slowly empties, as complete strangers carry away his tools in exchange for an operation for his wife that might not even work. He wonders what it must feel like to liquidate everything, to empty yourself like that. He thinks about that cavernous shop, once so complete, and wonders what it would feel like to begin again.

SATISFACTION GUARANTEED

YOU WERE HAPPY ONCE. To that I can testify. You were a happy baby. You would coo and gurgle and grab onto my finger as if it were a toy. You were happy for a long time. There's that picture of you at the Boy Scout Jamboree that Mother kept on her bureau. You're standing next to a picnic table in your freshly pressed Boy Scout uniform. There's a sash of merit badges across your chest and you're holding a hatchet. You were happy then. And after that, for a long time you were happy; you didn't have any reason not to be.

But then you started writing those letters and now you whore yourself to your lovers, to your alcohol, to your pursuit of anything you can get for nothing. Now when you call me in the early morning I can hear the terror in your voice. I can imagine your hair slicked in sweat, your fingertips stained yellow from chain smoking, your ribs poking through your shirt like branches.

When you call I still come, but I won't forever. Blood may be thicker than water, but even blood eventually dries up. In response to your sickness I have developed a theory about the angels, but you won't have any of it. It's so like you not to notice something that's right under your nose. I drive to your house through a light mist, the traffic lights still flashing, throwing red and yellow mirages on the wet pavement at the intersections. I notice the rain hanging on a green chain-link, like dew on a spider's web.

When I enter Dogtown I slow down and coast the narrow streets like a patrol car. Despite the depravity, I remember with fondness the year I spent living with you. I didn't move out to escape the ruins, but because you had become unbearable. To be fair, I stuck it out for months, but then one day you lashed out at me for buying fruit that wasn't guaranteed, and I found an apartment behind the high school.

I turn down your street and hear dogs barking in the distance. The yards on your street are strewn with eggshells, Styrofoam cups, magazines and empty cereal boxes. The picket fences need paint and have gaping holes, like missing teeth, where pickets have fallen off or have been stolen by kids for baseball bats. The houses are missing shingles and sometimes large sections of siding, exposing pink insulation or hollow walls. Porches are rotting away, hanging lazily on the fronts of the houses like swollen lips. It is a neighborhood of welfare mothers and students. It's Gothic and grim, and yet something about it made my leaving reluctant.

The angels are tied up in the backyards. Someone has tied them to the earth with heavy chains and studded collars. You see them when you go out to get the paper, or when you come home drunk at night, stumbling into the bushes. You see them at the edge of your vision like small pieces of trash on a mountain trail. You know you should stoop and pick them up, but something holds you back, and just like you ignore public service announcements and food additives, you ignore dogs. You are blind to what they really are.

I park on the street in front of your house and walk in the door. Inside it is still and dark. I turn on a light and see your desk littered with your "unhappy letters." The sight of them fills me with dread and gives me flu-like symptoms. These letters, this campaign, is the whole reason for my moving out. I want to go back outside, to run through the backyards releasing the angels, burying my hands in the thick fur at the back of their necks, but then I hear your choked voice from the kitchen.

I remember how it began. We were walking home from the local 7-Eleven. You had a bag of popcorn and I had a six-pack. We were halfway home when you grabbed me hard on the arm above the elbow and told me to look.

"What?" I said.

"Look at this," you said, your voice starting to tremble.

"What?" I said again.

"Read this," you said, handing me the bag and pointing to the back.

Our Guarantee

The Davis Family has been associated with the snack food industry over 25 years. Because of the pride we have in our products, we extend you this guarantee – If you find anything unacceptable about our product, just return the unused portion along with why you are unhappy with the product, and we will gladly refund your purchase price plus postage.

"So what?" I said.

But you had no patience for me. You began jumping around, elated.

"Anything unacceptable," you screamed.

"Why you're unhappy," you bellowed.

Popcorn bounced from the bag and fell to the ground.

"It's totally subjective," you cried. "We could eat for free for the rest of our lives!"

I reached to touch your shoulder, but you leapt away.

"You don't get it, do you?" you said. "I could be unhappy for any reason. I could say I was eating their caramel corn and my hamster died, and that made me unhappy, and they'd have to give me my money back. I could say their holiday mix reminded me of a vacation we took to the beach where I lost my favorite beach ball in the surf, and that made me unhappy. I could say their cheese curls stained my fingers yellow and reminded me of death, and that made me real unhappy, and they'd have to reimburse me. Do you see?"

"Sure," I said.

"And look," you said, grabbing my arm again.

I read again.

Other Fine Products

Cheese Puffs
Cheese Curls
Cheese Balls

"Cheese puffs! Cheese curls! Cheese balls!" you chanted maniacally. "The possibilities are endless!"

As soon as we were home, you launched your campaign. You reveled in coming up with creative ways to describe your unhappiness.

Dear Davis Snack Food Company,
   I have recently been made unhappy by one of your products. One day I bought a bag of your popcorn and was planning to go home and eat it with a beer or two while watching the baseball game on TV. However, the popcorn turned out to be very salty, and instead of

> drinking only one or two beers, as I had
> planned, I drank eleven (it was very salty).
> Consequently, I became violent with my poor
> wife who later divorced me. This has made me
> very unhappy.

They sent your money back along with four bags of low-salt pretzel sticks, which we ate on the front porch with a bottle of cheap champagne in celebration. After that you went crazy. You sent back snack food and everything else that had a guarantee on it. Before long you were completely obsessed. You wouldn't buy anything that you couldn't return for a full refund after eating all but a few pieces of. You returned snack food, fast food, even canned food. Soon you were returning books, clothes, toothpaste and shampoo, even running shoes. You ordered anything with a free trial period and sent it back after using it for thirty days. You got luggage, videotapes, exercise machines, and kitchen utensils. You took cars for long test drives. You had cable television installed one day and removed the next.

One day, late in the fall, I came home with a bag of fresh apples from Green Bluff, and you went through the roof. I moved out as soon as I found a place and two weeks later you cut off three fingers on your right hand with a chainsaw that had a "guaranteed safe" guard on it. At the hospital I sat by your bed looking at your bandaged hand and wondered what to do.

"Go away," you said. "I'm not crazy. I cut two cords of wood with that buzzer and then got a full refund on it.

You think that's crazy? It's genius."

I looked away and saw our rounded reflection on the dark TV hanging in the corner. Beyond the door was the rhythmic clicking of a woman's high heels slowly fading down the hall.

Days later I find you in your kitchen spread-eagle on your back, staring up at the ceiling. There's a Chesterfield between the two remaining fingers on your right hand, the smoke rising in slow motion, like electricity. I can tell you haven't slept all night. The sun is coming up, slanting through the window, and it picks up the dust in the air, the smoke from your cigarette.

I sit in a chair in the corner. I think about what I must say. How I must convince you that there are angels all around us—in the fields, in the streams, in our own backyards. How can I convince you that there really are no guarantees in life? That that's going about things all wrong, that the trick is to see the angels, all around us, and to realize they want good for us.

JESUS' TWIN

ON THE DAY before Thanksgiving Cassie appears at my bedroom door just as I'm finishing packing, although I haven't heard the front door open. She leans on the door jamb with her arms crossed and looks at me in the way she does, both superior and self-righteous, but also with a little sympathy, as if I'm someone that allowances need to be made for. There's a wintry light in the room that hovers between us like mist.

Don't do that, I say.

Do what?

What you're doing.

What am I doing?

Okay, forget it. Are you ready to go?

As ready as you are.

I carry my suitcase out onto the front landing and Cassie follows. When I put the suitcase down to lock the door Cassie surprises me by picking it up. I watch her for a moment as she walks down the steep cement steps to the parking lot. I wonder what she's playing at, if anything at all. Sometimes it's impossible to think of her as my twin, because we're so different, but now I notice she's cut her hair in a way that's a lot like mine. She's wearing my boots, or boots I've worn in the past. She's also not wearing any makeup, but this could be a concession for Mother.

We get into my new Volvo and Cassie runs her hand across the leather.

Nice.

She says it in a way that only Cassie can, but I choose to ignore her.

Thank you.

I turn the key and pull out of the parking lot, but Cassie keeps inspecting the car.

Can you afford this?

I bought it, didn't I?

Did you get that promotion at work?

Not yet, but I'm going to.

What if you don't?

I will.

But what if you don't?

I will.

If you don't get it, you'll have to sell the car.

I won't have to sell the car, because I'm going to get the promotion, I say evenly.

Cassie shrugs and turns on the radio. She tunes it to a hip-hop station, but as soon as her hand is away I retune it to NPR. Cassie looks at me with mild amusement then tunes it back to her station. I put both hands on the wheel and drive. I don't care. I don't care what we listen to. I don't know what I'm in the mood for anyway.

Late morning and the city streets are quiet. I imagine a lot of people have already left for the holidays. Cassie says they're just sleeping in. The sky is sharkskin gray and the clouds are beginning to press down. We hadn't planned on going home for Thanksgiving this year, but when our father called and told us about the latest incident with Mother how could we refuse? Having our mother for a mother is a lot like having a piece of salad stuck in your front teeth: Some people will politely bring it to your attention, others will act like it isn't there. Cassie says it's more like genital odor. And most people *won't* bring that to your attention, although they'll be damned well aware of it.

Cassie remembers this latest incident, or rather Father's *retelling* of it, differently than I do. Cassie says that they were at a Halloween party and Mother came home with a pair of pearl earrings. I'll concede that it was a Halloween party, but it wasn't pearl earrings. It was someone's watch. And a set of pewter salt and pepper shakers, too. Whatever it was it's plainly a cry for help, just like her therapist suggested, although it's never been clear what kind of help she's crying for. What I don't understand is how our presence is deemed helpful. Father says she wants us there, that it's not Thanksgiving without us, but we seem to have lost the ability to communicate with each other.

Just before getting onto the interstate Cassie points to a liquor store and commands me to pull over. I stop in the deserted parking lot and look at her.

What?

Let's get a bottle of wine for the drive.

It's ten-thirty in the morning.

Oh, she says. You've never needed a glass of wine before noon.

No, not needed.

Wanted.

I don't have a corkscrew.

I'll get the kind with the screw cap.

Before I can object she's out of the car and trotting across the parking lot. She has a nice figure, slimmer in the hips than me, looks better in jeans than me. I'm not much bigger, but my weight tends to pendulum a bit, from right where I want to be (like Cassie), to a few pounds beyond.

Cassie comes back with a bottle in a brown paper sack. I hope she hasn't gotten something stronger than wine, but no, it's just wine. She pulls it from the paper sack, unscrews the cap and takes a sip. She hands it to me and I put it between my legs while I navigate out of the parking lot and back onto the highway. When I get onto the interstate I take a sip and hand the bottle back to Cassie. I'll admit I wouldn't mind being a little more relaxed when we get to Mother's, but Cassie ends up drinking most of the bottle.

There's not much traffic on the interstate. The trees on either side of the road have dropped their leaves and a fine snow is beginning to fall through the bare branches. Cassie hands me the bottle and I take another sip. Despite the screw top it's good wine. As different as we are, we usually agree on wine.

After about half an hour I'm feeling more relaxed than I wanted and I inadvertently start a conversation that I told myself in the morning that I wouldn't.

I can't believe Mother's stealing again.

Cassie gives a little snort through her nose, something I find unattractive and wish she wouldn't do.

I can't believe she got caught, she says.

What's that supposed to mean?

Cassie twirls a strand of hair around her finger and looks at me. She wants a cigarette, but knows it's not even worth asking with the new car. She thinks I'm naïve and maybe I am.

Oh, come on Callie. Do you really think Mother ever stopped stealing?

I thought the therapy...

The therapy was a joke. She stole pens from the guy's desk.

How do you know that?

I found them in her purse. You know that as well as I do, because I showed them to you.

I don't remember.

Well, I did. How convenient that you forgot.

Are you sure you told me?

I told you.

When the wine is gone Cassie puts her head back and closes her eyes. I feel like doing the same, but I concentrate on the line in the middle of the road and pinch my earlobes, which I think I remember hearing once is an acupressure point that's supposed to keep you awake. Or, maybe it's to relieve menstrual cramps, I can't be sure. It's probably something I heard from Father, which would tend to make it suspect in either case.

When I pull down my parents' street Cassie opens her eyes. There are piles of leaves raked up in the yards, bags of them standing at the curbs. Already some of the neighbors have put out Christmas decorations. There's a Santa and sled and eight reindeer on the peak of someone's roof, but thankfully my parents at least have the good taste to wait until after Thanksgiving. I pull into the driveway and stop in front of the double garage. I watch my hand push the gearshift into park, but it seems like someone else's hand, like a hand that's not connected to me.

Jesus, I think. How did I let myself get this drunk?

I look at Cassie. I want to give her a pat on the knee, make some kind of physical contact, show her that we're in this together, but my hand stays where it is on the gearshift.

Are you ready? she says.

I nod, but even this little movement seems a risk to

my equilibrium.

Mother meets us at the door. She takes our hands and kisses us on the cheek then takes a step back to size us up. She'll think Cassie is too skinny. Me, she'll find dangerously plump. She won't say anything, but we'll see it in her eyes. Neither of us has ever received a compliment that wasn't a shrouded criticism.

Well, she says. She stands up on the balls of her feet and peeks over our shoulders. Are the boys bringing in the luggage?

I want to go to bed. It's easier to have parents when you have a boyfriend. I can already see that this whole weekend is going to be too much. But Cassie handles it. She takes off her coat and heads for the kitchen.

There aren't any boys, she says. We ditched them, remember? We told you weeks ago.

Mother is wearing a flowered apron over a cream silk blouse. She smoothes the front of it with her hands as if someone else has just come to the door. She waits a moment then follows Cassie into the kitchen. I wander alone through the living room, but I can hear them talking.

That nice Todd? He adored you.

He could barely spell his last name, says Cassie.

You don't have to be vindictive, says Mother.

I can hear Mother picking something up and wiping it with the front of her apron, something that's already clean. Cassie opens the refrigerator and takes a sip of juice from the carton.

What about that Andy? says Mother.

There's a long moment of silence then the refrigerator door clicks shut.

That was Callie's boyfriend, says Cassie. And *he* broke up with *her*. I wouldn't bring it up. She still cries whenever she thinks about him.

Dear, says Mother. I don't know what it is with you girls. You break up with the ones who adore you and the ones you adore break up with you. It wasn't like this when I was a girl. Things were simpler then.

A horse is simpler than a car, says Cassie. That doesn't mean it's better.

I put my hand on the smooth wood of the balustrade. My temples ache and my tongue is dry. I hear Father moving around in the basement, tinkering with his homemade wine, which we pretend to drink out of politeness but which tastes like fabric softener. I haven't been down in the basement for years. Father refuses to wear deodorant because he says it causes Alzheimer's. He believes Jesus had a twin who continued the carpentry business and lived to be a hundred and six. He once told me that if you fell asleep under a black locust you'd never wake up. You wouldn't die; you'd just never wake up. Mother is always accusing him of filling the world with preposterous ideas, but I think she misses the point. I tend to believe the things Father says. If not always the factuality of them, then at least the underlying spirit. Ironically, I'd have to say that of the two of them, he's the sane one.

I climb the stairs as quickly as I dare and go to my room. For a moment I stand in the middle of the floor and look around. It looks exactly the way it did the day I moved out. Maybe just a little cleaner. I pull back the covers of the bed and climb in still wearing my coat. I lie on my side and hug my knees up to my chest. I wish Cassie would go a little easier on Mother. I wish she could understand that this is the way she loves us. That she's doing it the only way she knows how.

I remember a time years ago when things were different. I was walking home from school, feeling sick to my stomach, when I felt a warm fluid begin to run down the inside of my legs. It was my first period, but I didn't know that then. It was the kind of thing my mother found easier to deal with when the time came, not before. She eventually found me in the upstairs bathroom where she'd heard me crying. I thought that there was something drastically wrong with me—ovarian cancer or a ruptured uterus—but at the same time I felt strangely ashamed. A little dirty. I didn't want to let her in.

But her voice had something in it I didn't quite recognize. I think now it was compassion. And I was more scared than ashamed, so I let her in.

She knelt on the tile floor next to me and took my hand.

Oh honey, she said. It's nothing to be afraid of. You just got your Monthly Visitor.

She made it sound like almost a privilege and I immediately felt better. She got me some aspirin and some tampons from her bathroom and showed me what to do. She even cried a little because I wasn't her little girl any more. We spent the rest of the afternoon in the kitchen together baking cookies and when my father came in she shooed him away and told him that we girls needed to be alone.

Whenever people ask me about my mother that's what I want to tell them about, not all the other stuff. For years afterward, whenever Cassie and I would get our periods, and we always got them at the same time, we would speak of our Monthly Visitor arriving. And it felt good to do that.

But now I'm left with the courtesies I've failed to acknowledge. The kindnesses I've failed to recognize or belittled. The fits I've pitched for no good reason. The lies I've told and the resentments I've nursed. In truth I'm just a spiteful ingrate who's waited a bit too long to grab the chance to make amends.

I've never done for my parents the things attentive and caring children do. I've never thrown them lavish anniversary parties or sent them on cruises, flown in far-flung relatives at my own expense, arranged for sentimental Mother's Day extravaganzas. I've never even offered to take my mother out to lunch.

I wake up to the sound of shattering glass. For a moment I can't tell if I really heard it or if it was part of some half-remembered dream. But then the voices rise from below like bees coming out of a hive.

Is this what we've come to? says Mother.

Give me a break, says Cassie. It was an accident.

You've always hated that platter. I heard you and Callie talking about it last Thanksgiving. You said it looked like a troglodyte.

Okay! screams Cassie. Have it your way! I did it on purpose! I couldn't stand to look at it any more so I dropped it on your beautiful faux tile linoleum floor!

It was a wedding gift, says Mother.

I bet they still make them, says Cassie. Why don't you just go out and steal another one?

There's a long silence then I hear my mother's even voice.

Why do you hate me?

Because you want me to! You've always wanted me to. So you can feel sorry for yourself! So you won't have to be my mother! So you can act like a victim!

I put my hands over my ears, but I can hear Cassie stomping out of the kitchen and down the hallway. At the bottom of the stairs she runs into Father who, unaware that anything has happened, offers her a glass of his homemade wine.

No! screams Cassie. I don't want any of your wine! It tastes like Downy!

The front door slams and the storm windows rattle. I get up and go to the frosted glass and see Cassie walking down the street in nothing but her thin cashmere sweater. Buster, my father's German shepherd, is trotting along behind, glad that someone has decided to take a walk. I run down the stairs and grab her coat and follow her out into the cold. I call to her, and I know she must hear, but she doesn't slow down. I finally catch up to her at a vacant lot at the end of the street. Cassie is standing knee deep in ocher grass spangled with frost. There's a cat intensity in her eyes. I touch the fine weave of her sweater and place the coat over her shoulders. Cassie looks at me, her eyes glistening.

Why am I like this Callie? Why can't I be more like you?

We have to try to understand her. We have to make allowances.

I don't want to make allowances. She's my mother. I shouldn't have to take care of her. Who's going to take care of me?

I put my arms around Cassie and hug her. Her body is cold and thin.

There's forgiveness, I say.

I feel Cassie's body tremble.

I don't need forgiveness, she murmurs into my shoulder.

I stroke the hair at the back of her head then Buster barks and snarls and tears into something on the ground several feet away. Cassie and I rush over and pull Buster away, but it's already too late. Buster has gotten into a nest of baby rabbits. A few are dead already, but a handful of others are writhing with open wounds. I kneel in the rough grass, but Cassie puts a hand on my shoulder and stops me.

What are you doing? she asks.

Shouldn't we take them home? Try to save them?

Don't be ridiculous. They wouldn't make it anyway.

But we have to do something.

Yes, says Cassie.

What are you going to do? I ask.

Put them out of their misery. Stomp on their heads.

You can't.

We have to.

I turn my head as Cassie raises her boot above the bunnies but I can't shut out the sound of crunching bones. Cassie stomps and stomps, way beyond what is reasonable for the task. I can't help feeling she's thinking of those bunnies as something else entirely. I feel myself enclosed in an ermine cocoon and no longer hear Buster's frenetic barking. I feel myself slipping, tracking backward, growing younger, and wondering if I continue on this path will I eventually come to that place, that point, where everything began to go wrong? I wonder, too, if I will recognize it.

Cassie and I walk arm in arm back down the street. There's a moment of quiet indecision as we stand in the driveway and look at the blurred house, the tears in our eyes like a saline drip. This is the house we grew up in; it should feel like home, a place to come back to. Instead it feels stained and cold and unalive. I know we should go in, that we should make some attempt at reconciliation, that my mother is doing the best she can, that things have happened that we're not aware of. But suddenly it all seems so hopeless. I think this must be the way depressed people feel about simple tasks like doing the dishes or making the bed. Why do them at all when the next day they'll just be dirty and unmade again? In the end we get into the car and drive silently away. As we get onto the interstate and head south I look at Cassie for the first time.

Is this one of the unforgivable sins? I ask. Arriving for Thanksgiving but leaving before it begins?

Cassie stares out the window at a frayed wire fence on the edge of the black and white woods.

Maybe, she says. Maybe it is.

I don't see Cassie much anymore. After Mother died I didn't seem to have as much need of her. Mother's death took away that need for anger. What good is it being angry at a ghost? Sometimes I look in the mirror and I can see traces of Cassie, but the similarities are what I like least about myself. And Cassie was wrong. We do need forgiveness. We need to forgive and we need to be forgiven. Maybe most of all we need to forgive ourselves; maybe that's the hardest thing.

Perhaps I had a twin once, I don't know, she was real enough to me. But now I know it was me that said and did those things all those years ago and I have to live with that, and live with the fact that I never got to ask for Mother's forgiveness. Maybe she wouldn't have granted it, I don't know. But still, I think the asking would have been enough. Because when I stand before God and am weighed on the scales and found wanting, it won't be any of the other bad things I've done in my life. It won't be stomping those rabbits; it will be that troglodyte platter. That goddamn troglodyte platter and how I said she could steal another one.

A CLEAR SIGN OF THE END

TO CELEBRATE their mother's 75th birthday the extended Hamilton family (eighteen of them) rent a 400-year-old hacienda high in the Andes mountains of Colombia. Their mother had been born in Bogotá to missionary parents, but she hadn't been back to Colombia since she was ten. This was what she'd wanted for her birthday, to see Colombia again, to have her family with her, although the children had their doubts whether she would recognize any of it. The hacienda was a place her parents sometimes went for short vacations, a place famous then and still today for raising very mediocre fighting bulls. When she went there with her parents they would arrive with a cardboard suitcase full of dried pasta, flour and beans. On this trip they will eat in the hacienda's restaurant, a large, high-ceilinged room with dark wainscoting that runs six feet up the walls and a stone fireplace at each end, and a menu that sports fresh shoyu ahi poki, raw oysters, candied pork ribs, and a 16-ounce Colombian cowboy rib steak served with a fresh horseradish demi.

In the late afternoon, freshly disembarked from their shuttle, Alison and Rick stand in front of the hacienda, its façade large and looming, like a face peering out of the jungle. The air is hot and sweet and full of the scent of things growing. They haven't talked much on the three-hour ride up from Bogotá, Alison's demeanor taciturn and weary, maybe resigned. She hadn't wanted to do this, had thought it an exercise in futility, but now here they are, among the coffee plantations, the banana trees, the spreading palms and the baking heat, and Rick is filled with hope bordering on euphoria. He'd known all along that if he could just get her here things would change. All they needed was a new perspective, a little time away to sort things out.

Alison and Rick had met two years earlier, during the 2002 evacuation of Portland. For months seismologists had been keeping an eye on Mount Hood, a volcano dormant for 300 years but, like a hibernating bear in spring, was now slowly coming back to life. For weeks they'd been watching billows of steam rising from the snow-capped crater above the serrated skyline of the city, but no one believed anything could actually happen. Biblically proportioned natural disasters were reserved for other times and other places.

Rick was single at the time, had been for six months, and it was something he was learning to be content with. His last girlfriend, Sarah, although almost a perfect clone of Meg Ryan, was not even remotely suited to him, nor he to her, although they both shared a love of pumpkin crème brûlée which was only available in Portland restaurants during the weeks between Thanksgiving and Christmas, a fact that together they decided was an unpardonable crime. They stayed together out of inertia, and because they rarely argued, until she finally broke the deadlock by dating her dentist who used, in Rick's opinion, the most inexcusable of lines on her, that she had perfect teeth. They parted on good terms, however, Sarah even giving Rick the present she'd bought for his birthday, which was still several weeks off. It was, most fittingly, a crème brûlée torch.

The evacuation order was issued on a Friday afternoon. For a few moments the whole city stood in hushed silence, as if the entire population was listening in concert for a telling creak or groan from the mountain. Then, like a frozen pipe thawing, the exodus began.

Moments later Rick was walking down Willamette Boulevard in a pumped-up throng of people, both anxious and excited. Everyone, in general, was very polite and courteous given the circumstances. Someone stepped on Rick's foot and immediately touched him on the arm and apologized. It was true that the city's continued existence was questionable, but on the other hand nothing like this had ever happened before. And, everyone was in it together.

The air was soft and warm and held a profound dreamlike quiet, as if the whole city were encased in an insular layer of fleece. The trees were blooming and there was a gentle southerly breeze. Rick looked up at the yellowing sky striated with a layer of cirrus. Then, in front of him on the sidewalk, amidst the sea of people coming and going, was a beautiful woman walking toward him. He'd never seen her before, but their eyes met, and as they passed each other, their heads turned. Rick could see the beginning of a smile forming on her face, and as they continued walking and turning, things got strange. She stopped. Rick couldn't break the gaze, and he stopped, too. They faced each other with only ten or fifteen feet between them. The crowd continued to pulse and surge around them, but Rick's field of vision was narrowed. All he saw was her.

Rick took a step or two forward, closing the distance between them. They were both smiling, both staring. When he was only a few feet in front of her, he stopped.

"Who are you?" he asked.

"Alison," she said. "What's going on?"

"I don't know," Rick said. "But I think we better go have coffee."

"Okay," she said.

Up in their room Alison goes into the bathroom and splashes water on her face. Rick tries the bed then pushes open the latticed doors that lead to a small balcony. The balcony looks out over an intimate garden with wooden benches and patinaed sculptures. The hills beyond are covered in dense green vegetation. Overhead, vultures rise on thermals like bits of ash rising from a fire.

Rick turns back inside and sits on the edge of the bed where Alison has flopped down face first. He puts his hand on the small of her back and feels the heat press into his palm.

"Do you want to go for a walk?" he asks.

Alison makes a sound down in her throat.

"I think I want to rest awhile."

Rick looks toward the balcony and sees a lizard skitter across the wall. It moves up above the door and pauses, its skin blending with the pale khaki wallpaper.

"Okay," he says. "I think I'll walk around a bit."

He kisses the back of Alison's head and goes downstairs. The tiled lobby is empty save for a wirehaired griffon stretched out like a horse in the entryway. Rick finds a door bordered by potted rubber plants that leads out to the garden he'd seen from his balcony. He can see now that the sculptures are of saints, robed and hooded and pious, although he couldn't say which ones. He looks up to the balcony where a slight breeze is ruffling the curtains on either side of the door. He hopes Alison is sleeping. She'll feel better after a nap. Then he'll come back and they'll have a cocktail together before meeting the family.

Rick finds a path that leads out of the garden and through a grove of trees, their lower branches covered in hanging vines. He wonders what kinds of lizards and snakes lurk there. After a while the trees open up onto a grassy field full of a violet flower that he guesses might be lavender. The sun is searing, baking, he can feel it turning the marrow of his bones to magma. But he feels that same euphoric calm he's been feeling ever since he arrived. All of this, the heat, the smells, the lush vegetation, is telling him something, and although he doesn't know what it is yet, he knows it's good.

Something moves on the other side of the clearing. A flock of small black birds evacuates a tree and streaks across the sky like a wave. But it wasn't the birds that caught his attention. There'd been something else first, something moving on the ground at the edge of the trees. Rick shields his eyes and looks out over the grass. Was it a person? Rick walks across the clearing, the grass rough on his bare shins. When he gets to the other side he enters the shade of the trees and crouches down.

"Hello?"

The trees have low branches and gnarled limbs. The bark flakes off like the wrapper of a cigar.

"Hello?"

Whatever it was, if it was anything, is gone now. Rick stands up and wipes the sweat from his forehead, and begins circling back to the hacienda. He's started thinking that a shower would be nice before having that cocktail with Alison.

Of course Rick and Alison never got their coffee. In the heat of their primal attraction they'd forgotten that the city was in a state of evacuation. They tried a Starbucks and then another Starbucks right across the street, but they found the doors already locked, the OPEN signs flipped over to CLOSED. They stood on the sidewalk for a moment and continued their locked-gaze dance in the cocoon that had wrapped itself around them. They'd said only a few words to each other up until then, but it was clear to both of them by that point that there was no alternative but to evacuate together. Her car was parked nearby and in a moment they were driving north on 205 toward the Columbia. It was slow going at first, but time had lost its meaning. Alison reached over and touched the back of Rick's hand and an electrical current coursed across his scalp. A moment later he found himself touching her arm. By nightfall the traffic had thinned and they sped through the night with their hands clasped together over the console, the strange dance beguiling to both of them, but also as inevitable as gravity.

Alison drove them to her father's hunting cabin in southern Idaho. By the time they arrived they'd heard on the radio that seismic activity had been recorded twelve miles off the coast of Washington. There was lava spewing across the ocean floor, the steam rising to the surface like a hot springs. This activity had somehow released enough seismic pressure that seismologists no longer thought Mount Hood was a candidate for eruption. But Alison and Rick were in no hurry to return to the city. She unlocked the front door of the cabin and led him inside.

* * *

The next morning Rick wakes up with a slight buzzing in his head, as if he's already had several cups of the strong Colombian coffee they've been drinking since entering the country. The room is still in deep morning shadow. Alison sleeps face down next to him, naked except for a pair of ankle socks with a light-blue border. The sheet is pulled down to her hips exposing her back, tanned and taut. Rick touches the declivity between her shoulder blades and is surprised by how cool her skin is, but Alison doesn't stir. He tries to remember if they made love the night before, but finds he can't. Dinner itself is a hazy memory. Did one of his brothers produce a bottle of Macallans afterward? Rick has a vague memory of looking across the common room at Alison talking to one of his sisters, pleased that they seemed to be getting along so well.

Rick leaves Alison to sleep. Downstairs he pokes his head into the dining room. No one else is up yet, but there's an urn of fresh coffee and a platter of fruit laid out on one of the tables. He pours himself some coffee and wanders outside, and without really thinking about it, soon finds himself on the same path he'd taken the afternoon before. The morning air is soft and light, and full of the sound of birdsong. He thinks the cup of coffee might be the best he's ever tasted. His whole body feels massaged and loose, not hung over, which he suspects he might be. When he gets to the meadow of lavender he scares up two fawns that have been bedding down there. They skip quickly into the woods, their white spots blurring in Rick's vision like shooting stars. Had this been what he'd seen the day before? One of the fawns? He didn't think so.

When he gets to the other side of the clearing he ducks into the woods and sees what he'd failed to notice the day before—that the path continues. He walks along it, the ground soft and loamy under his feet, the canopy above dense and green and protective. After about twenty minutes the trees give way to another clearing. This one is spotted with delicate blue flowers that sway in the morning breeze. In the middle of the clearing sits a small white house with a stone foundation. Rick immediately thinks of the gamekeeper's house in *Lady Chatterley's Lover*. He thinks of Alison back at the hacienda, probably still sleeping, and for the first time he allows himself to doubt. What if all this really is an exercise in futility? What if when they get back to the city they find that nothing has changed? What if the trip to Colombia is nothing more than a cortisone shot, something that gives relief for a while, but eventually wears off?

Alison and Rick's first argument came a month after they met. It was really nothing more than a disagreement. Alison claimed they'd stayed at the hunting cabin in Idaho for a day and a half. Rick was sure it was closer to a week. It was such a minor thing, almost laughable, and they did laugh. But it was also bothersome. Alison couldn't understand how Rick could have gotten it so wrong, and Rick thought the same. He could concede that it might have been a little less than a week, but a day and a half? Was she taking drugs? Was she supposed to be taking drugs and stopped?

That little episode quickly slipped into oblivion. The fact was, they felt they had entered into something that doesn't happen very often. Since returning to Portland nothing had been the same. Rick didn't want things to be the same. He wanted to rearrange his whole life, open that restaurant he'd always dreamed of, buy a house, and revamp his personality from criminally unambitious to fervently optimistic. And he wanted Alison at the center, to be his nucleus, that hot, dense gravitational point around which everything else revolved.

One night he told her he wanted to buy a house.

"With you," he said, "I don't feel like a renter any more."

A week later a real estate agent called and described a prospective house. He spoke glowingly of its many features—the large yard, the new roof, and the nice neighborhood—but hinted that the house had one problem. He assured Rick that the matter would not be difficult considering his renovation skills, but he refused to offer details until Rick could tour the house.

At the time Rick was working on a kitchen remodel on the West Side where the houses are tiered up from the river like grape terraces. He'd finished the floor, cabinets and most of the trim. About all that was left was the installation of the granite countertops, but the countertops hadn't arrived and Rick was running out of things to do. He called Alison at work in the middle of the afternoon and asked if she could get away and come look at the house.

They met the real estate agent on the front steps. Before letting them in he told them that several potential buyers had fallen in love with the house, but then balked at making an offer when they discovered the flaw. They went in and found that much of the house suffered from a 1950s and '60s color scheme. In the kitchen, a pineapple-yellow refrigerator fought for attention with an avocado dishwasher, but the layout was comfortable. Alison took Rick's arm and whispered into his ear.

"I like it."

But they hadn't gotten to the fatal flaw. That was to be found in the master bathroom. The real estate agent opened the door to the bathroom and stood aside to let them have their own unbridled reactions. Rick felt Alison's pulse quicken in his hand.

Everything was pink. The walls, the ceiling, the tile around the tub, the shag carpet and the toilet seat were all blazing pink. Even the toilet, sink and bathtub were pink. Everything was in perfect shape and fully functional, but the whole room glowed pink as if it were powered by a hidden reactor.

"Well," said the real estate agent.

He went outside to make a phone call and give them a few minutes to look around. Alison and Rick closed the door to the bathroom and went back downstairs. They stood at the large windows of the living room and watched as a listing sailboat cut across the slice of view they had of the river. Alison put her arm around Rick's waist and he breathed in a strand of her hair.

"I've never been a pink kind of girl," said Alison.

Rick looked at her and kissed her forehead.

"I've never really been slain by it either."

But the price was right and everything else about the house was perfect, so Rick bought it and moved in. Alison kept her apartment for several months, but when all her plants died she let it go. They both assumed that Rick would get right to the bathroom, but he'd always found it easier to work on other people's projects, and he'd always relied on other people to take the initiative.

Rick approaches the little house, the blue flowers swaying mystically below his knees. There's a single tree in the meadow, large and thick-limbed, some kind of nut tree Rick guesses. The morning is warming up quickly, but the air in this meadow still has a buoyancy to it. Rick decides that he must bring Alison here. She would like the quaintness of the little house and find the flowers beautiful. Maybe the cook at the hacienda could put a little picnic basket together for them. Rick is under the tree picking up a walnut when he hears the voice.

"Well?"

Rick is good with accents. Even with just the one word he's sure this one is Australian, maybe Kiwi. Rick palms the walnut and turns. An old woman stands at the back door in a housedress. She's one of those women who have aged beyond definition, for years shrinking and withering, folding up, as if she's planning to return to the womb. Rick smiles and holds out his hand.

"Excuse me," he says. "I was just noticing the

walnuts."

It's an idiotic thing to say but the woman doesn't seem to notice.

"Yes, yes, I'll get you a bag for those later, but first you must come in for tea."

She turns back into the house, leaving the door ajar, and Rick is compelled to follow. He finds himself in a little kitchen, cluttered with newspapers and mail and dirty dishes. There's a small brick fireplace with a pile of unlit coal on its grate. The old woman hunches at the sink, filling a copper kettle.

"Sit," she says, glancing over her shoulder.

Rick doesn't see anywhere to sit. There's a kitchen table with two chairs, but both table and chairs are covered in detritus, the detritus layered with coal dust. When she's lit the stove and situated the kettle the old woman sees Rick still standing near the door. There's really nowhere else to go. But the woman quickly clears off one of the chairs and just enough table space for a plate of cookies.

"I haven't been much of a housekeeper since Liam died," she says.

An hour later Rick and Alison are sitting on their little balcony with a bottle of rum and two bottles of coke. There's a metal bucket of ice under Alison's chair, which she reaches into periodically, sometimes adding ice to her drink, sometimes rubbing it on her neck and between her breasts. She had not seemed overly interested when Rick had started telling her about the old woman, but now she's listening.

Things had been normal enough at first. Just a lonely old woman, maybe a little eccentric, widowed and alone, but halfway through the cup of tea Rick realized that she was completely insane.

"It was like *A Rose for Emily*," he says. "I wouldn't be surprised if her husband is lying dead upstairs in their bed and that she sleeps with him every night. Remember the iron-gray hair? Her hair was just like that."

"You're the one who's insane," says Alison. "I think the heat is making you wacky."

"She kept going on about all her family—sons and daughters and grandchildren—how they're always visiting and taking her on outings, but I guarantee you she's alone. No one's been in that house but her for years."

Alison looks at Rick, squinting against the sun, then reaches under her chair for an ice cube and plops it into her drink.

"You're making all of this up," she says.

Rick tosses back the last of his drink then begins making a fresh one.

"You'll come with me tomorrow," he says.

On the night Alison moved in with Rick they went out to dinner at what is widely considered the best restaurant in Portland—Tabor Park. It was more than they could afford, but they were still high on the supernal dance they'd been performing since they met, and they wanted to celebrate in the midst of the music in case it ever stopped playing or changed tune. Looking back they'd both agree that even then, when the strange chemistry between them was at its most fevered pitch, they knew that someday it must.

After dinner they walked along the river. The night was clear and the sky was filled with pulsing stars. They passed a woman walking a schnauzer that was wearing a frilly sweater and they learned that aside from the obvious sexual attraction, they got along so well because they disapproved of the same things. Things like schnauzers in sweaters, buying sliced mushrooms instead of slicing your own, riding in a golf cart instead of walking, any person who would flush a live animal down a toilet and anyone, in general, who believed that global warming was a concept cooked up by left-wing radicals and didn't actually exist.

When Alison got cold they went into a little bistro that was trying very hard to be European and ordered pear ice cream and glasses of port. Alison asked Rick why he'd never opened his restaurant and Rick pretended to give it a moment of serious thought before he said, "I dunno."

They got back to the house late, fell into bed and made hasty love. Afterward Alison went to the bathroom, but she hadn't been in there long enough to do anything when she came back out and strolled downstairs. Rick heard the front screen door slam then, after a moment, heard what he thought was the lid of the toolbox in the back of his truck clanking shut. Alison came back in with a ten-pound sledge in one hand and a pair of goggles in the other. She was wearing nothing but a stringy camisole and her underwear, and the sight of her with a sledge hammer stirred Rick up enough to want to pull her back into bed and do it properly this time. He followed her into the bathroom and stood naked in the doorway while Alison took a full roundhouse swing. In an exciting shower of splinters and dust, she took out the sink, the medicine cabinet and a slice of several walls. With a reverse swing she knocked holes in the remaining walls, took out the light fixture, shattered the toilet, cracked the tile around the tub walls and put a significant dent in the ceiling. One more full swing in the near dark and the cast iron tub erupted with a nexus of cracks.

Suddenly sobered by the amount of dust and damage she'd created in such a short time, Alison stood still for a moment letting the sledge hang placidly at her side. She looked at Rick and wiped at her forehead with the back of her hand leaving a pink jet trail of dust.

"I'll get dressed," said Rick.

He put on work clothes and they toiled through the night. They pried up pink material—porcelain, drywall, tile fragments and fixtures—until they reached bare studs and subfloor. They hauled load after load of pink shrapnel out to the street. By the time they were done the eastern sky was beginning to show signs of turning pink, too. They dropped face first into bed fully dressed and fell asleep with the rosy dust still burning in their noses.

* * *

Alison doesn't go along the next day. She spends most of the night in the bathroom, either sitting on the toilet or puking into it. Rick suggests alcohol poisoning, but Alison insists she was well within her limits and blames the yellowfin she'd had for dinner that night. Just before dawn she finally crawls back into bed and Rick strokes her clammy thigh.

"Don't touch me," says Alison.

"Sorry."

"Don't talk, either," she says. "It makes me nauseous."

"I can't talk?"

"What, are you kidding me?"

Rick wants to talk. The day before he'd forgotten to tell Alison something else the woman had said, something that confirmed her insanity. He couldn't understand how he'd forgotten to mention it, and now he wasn't allowed to speak.

The old woman had told him that in 1938 her husband Liam had bought a brand new Studebaker. There was nothing inherently crazy about that. What was crazy, and what he wished he'd remembered to tell Alison, was that the old woman claimed she still had the car. It was parked in the garage behind the house. And, it was in mint condition.

"Oh yes," she'd said. "It was Liam's pride and joy. He'd give it a wash and put a coat of wax on it every Saturday. My kids tell me I should sell it, but I couldn't bear to part with it."

It was possibly true, but Rick was sure it wasn't. The

car, like the children and grandchildren, was a myth.

That morning he visits the old woman again, and again she invites him in for tea. The kitchen is still a mess, although Rick thinks there's been some attempt at straightening. What it amounts to, however, is moving things from one pile to another. When he'd first arrived she'd acted like she'd been expecting him, like popping in for tea was something he'd been doing for years, but this time she gave him a paper sack and asked him to gather walnuts while the tea was brewing.

Back at the hacienda he finds Alison in the garden sipping a gin and tonic.

"Hair of the dog?" he asks.

Alison looks at him disdainfully.

"It was food poisoning."

Rick regrets his comment. He doesn't want to argue. He wants to tell Alison more about the old woman.

"I'm sorry," he says. "Are you feeling better?"

"Better enough to drink one of these," she says. "But I'm still a little shaky. How's your crazy lady?"

"You'll have to come with me tomorrow," he says. "I've been trying to figure out a way to get upstairs so I can take a peek in the bedroom. If you were there I might be able to manage it."

"I'm not going to have anything to do with something like that."

"I'll just take a peak. If there's not a rotting corpse in the bed, we'll leave quietly."

"And what if there is?"

"Then I'll have been right and you'll have been wrong."

Alison shakes her head and takes a drink from her glass. Rick focuses on the lime, which is wedged halfway down in the ice, like something stuck in an iceberg.

"Is that what this is about?" says Alison.

Rick looks down, suddenly feeling childish.

"No," he says. "But I've been there. You just get this feeling."

"You just get this feeling that there's a rotting corpse in the house."

The way Alison says it makes it sound ludicrous which, Rick realizes, is exactly her intent. He suddenly wonders if there's anything salvageable here, or if he even wants to find out anymore. If cruelty creeps into a relationship, isn't that a clear sign of the end? He tries to think of the last time they laughed, really laughed together, and he has to go all the way back to the morning after they'd destroyed the bathroom, although he's sure there were others.

The morning after the bathroom demolition Rick and Alison woke up simultaneously and stretched under the covers. There was a dull ache in their backs and arms; their hands felt as though they'd spent the day rock climbing. Alison rolled over and Rick noticed that her eyebrows were still tinted with pink like a Vegas cocktail waitress. They fell out of bed and took turns showering in the downstairs bathroom, both of them unable to shake the strange feeling that something in the night had been accomplished, although whether it was good or bad remained elusive.

They decided to go out for breakfast. It was a bright, sunny day, the kind of day in Portland that incites strangers to talk to one another, the kind of day when people are more apt to have a chance encounter with someone in the park and wind up falling in love. Rick rolled down his window and backed out of the drive, past the pile of debris they'd piled at the edge of the street. He was halfway down the block before he stopped. Alison looked at him with an enigmatic expression, both perplexed and anticipatory. Rick put the car in reverse and returned to the driveway and the two of them gazed at the pile of bathroom debris in the morning sunlight.

The chunks of drywall, the medicine cabinet, the light fixtures, the rug and toilet seat cover were indeed pink. But the sink, the toilet, the tub and tile fragments were not pink at all, but a lovely soft beige. The epiphany arrived for both of them at the same time. The light from the pink light fixtures had ricocheted across the pink walls, the pink rug, and the pink shower curtain to overwhelm the room and make everything seem pink. They had needlessly destroyed the whole room and everything in it when all that was necessary was a fresh coat of paint and some new fixtures.

They ended up skipping breakfast. When they stopped laughing enough so it was safe to drive, they drove to a park and walked the path that meandered along the river. As the joggers and dog walkers passed by, Rick and Alison were encased in their own silent world, a world that was rare and where they were lucky, because they were aware they were lucky.

Rick and Alison lie side by side in bed and stare at a lizard lurking above them on the ceiling. The air in the room is hot and stale, and they're both thinking that unless a breeze kicks up it's going to be too hot to sleep. Might as well go downstairs and have another drink. They wouldn't have to be alone. There are probably others thinking the same thing. But then Alison reaches over and takes Rick's hand, and it's such an intimate gesture that Rick is torn between regaining a sliver of hope and wondering what she's up to.

"I'm sorry," says Alison.

Her voice is soft and sweet. She's not up to anything.

"For what?"

"You know. For being the way I've been."

An apology. Is this all that was needed? But Rick has misunderstood.

"I mean, we both know this isn't working out. That doesn't mean it has to get ugly. We care about each other. We should at least be able to salvage a friendship."

So that's it, thinks Rick. The end. He stares at the lizard and the lizard blinks. A numbness, almost akin to sexual arousal, washes over him. He's glad it happened here. It would have been worse in Portland, although he knows as soon as he gets home it's going to hurt like hell.

Alison gives a little squeeze and releases his hand. Then her voice comes out of the dim light like something from another era.

"Why don't you look for the car?"

"Look for the car?"

"The old woman's Studebaker. If it's there, wouldn't that prove she wasn't crazy? Wouldn't that be easier than sneaking into her bedroom?"

"There's no car," says Rick.

He realizes he wants to hurt her, the way she hurt him in the garden earlier. At the same time he wants to be big enough not to.

"What if there is?" asks Alison.

"A 1938 Studebaker? That they bought in 1938? And still in mint condition?"

"Okay," she says, rolling onto her side, "have it your way."

The looked-for breeze arrives, ruffling the curtains, taking the staleness from the room, and soon Alison's breathing is heavy and regular.

Rick lies there for a long time, hearing the lizard's feet scratching against the chipped paint. It's well into the night when he slips out of bed and gets dressed. The path to the old woman's house is bathed in moonlight, bright enough to cast bluish shadows in the lee of trees and bushes. Rick walks slowly, cautiously, not wanting to trip, but also not wanting to rush the journey. As he walks he wonders what he expects will happen. What does he want? Does he want the garage to be empty, or does he want to find the car? He doesn't know what either outcome will mean, only that Alison had been right and that he has to find out one way or the other.

The clearing where the old woman's house stands is bright with moonlight, but the garage's windows are shadowed with years of dust and it's so dark inside that Rick can't see anything. There's a serrated leafy plant growing at the base of the garage and it tears at Rick's ankles and shins as he circles the garage and looks for a way in. The front doors are fastened with a padlocked bolt, but on the far side he finds a small door, also padlocked, but which he is able to pull off its hinges and open the opposite way.

He has to duck through the short door and when he does that familiar garage smell—oil and metal shavings and dust—assaults his nostrils. And there is the car, lying there like a sleeping animal. As his eyes slowly adjust to the dim moonlight he can see that it is just as the old lady has described. Although it's covered in a thick layer of ash-like dust, he can see that it is indeed in mint condition, apparently not aged an iota from the day it was bought. He walks around and looks at the headlights, at the perfect chrome, at the tires that don't even show signs of dry rot. When he opens the driver's side door there is no aching creak of ungreased hinges. Everything is perfect. As he slides behind the wheel he notices the supple leather, like a baby's skin right after a bath. He puts his hands on the wheel and feels the smoothness of the molded plastic and he realizes that this, after all, had been what he'd been looking for.

The keys are in the ignition, dangling on a worn leather strap. Rick reaches out through the dreamlike light and closes his eyes as he touches the coolness of the key. A slight smile spreads across his face as he turns the key and thinks of Alison. But of course, nothing happens.

THE OFFICE

ALL OF US PRETEND to complain, because that's what you do. But in private conversations, with others we trust, maybe over a glass of Pinot Noir or a martini at a quiet fern bar, we all admit that the office is a good place to work.

At the office we work on flex time, which means we can pretty much come and go as we please as long as we're putting in the hours each week and getting the job done. Sometimes we show up early so we can leave early. Sometimes we arrive late and leave late. Sometimes we arrive late and leave early. We do this mostly on Fridays.

It may sound like anarchy, but it works. The boss is of the opinion that if you provide a safe and flexible work environment where the coffee is always on, then the employees will respond with respect and work responsibly. And we do. We get the job done. When there's a project due we hunker down and bang out the reports and order in pizzas and stay until everything is spit spot and ready. The boss can leave at five with no worries. He knows we'll be there for as long as it takes and when he comes in in the morning everything he needs will be on his desk, labeled and collated, color-coded and ready to go.

Part of the allure of the office, besides the flex time, is the care that's been taken to make it a safe work environment. Everyone in the office is acutely aware of the multitudinous hazards that await us at every one of life's turns, so it's a great comfort to know that at least while we're at work, which admittedly is a good portion of our lives, preventive measures have been taken. For example: City code mandates that an office space of our size and configuration must have two fire exits, but ours has three. They are red, clearly marked outward-opening doors with gray crash bars and well-greased hinges. They make all of us extremely confident that if there ever were a fire, which is very unlikely in the first place, we would have no trouble getting out in a safe and orderly fashion. We know this because periodically we have spontaneous pre-planned fire drills and they always come off without a hitch. The only hitch any of us can remember was when a young intern arrived at the office in the midst of a fire drill, after we'd all left the building, and being of a particularly fundamental religious persuasion took it into her head that the Rapture had taken place and she'd been left behind. Needless to say, she's no longer with the company.

It's indicative of the office to go a little beyond what's required, to go, as they say, the extra mile. Case in point: The office is also equipped with a state-of-the-art climate control system that keeps the ambient air temperature at a constant sixty-eight degrees while maintaining the humidity at forty-five percent. There are some in the office (quite a large majority, actually) that believe the humidity should be increased to fifty-five percent, but we also all know that forty-five percent is the ideal humidity for the delicate equipment we use, so no one brings it up at the risk of appearing not to be a team player. If there's one thing we've all learned it's that being a team player is one of the attributes the office values the most. That and the ability to think independently.

The office is also equipped with an air filtration system that eliminates dust, fungus and allergens down to .0006 microns. This essentially means that if a crop duster flew through the office spraying anthrax and DDT none of us would be the worse for wear. It's a good, clean place.

The office also supplies us with all the pens, pencils and company stationery a person could ever want, and although it's officially against company policy to use these items for personal use, it really falls into the don't-ask don't-tell category. There is at least one known case of an office employee who scripted an entire screenplay on office stationery and then proceeded to sell it to Hollywood. Needless to say, he's no longer with the company.

There are no less than a dozen good restaurants within walking distance of the office and whenever we aren't on deadline we make it a point to patronize them at lunch time as often as possible. These lunches are always relaxing and comfortable and well-attended. That wasn't always the case. There was a period when we hit a bumpy stretch (this would have been in the mid-nineties) when a dark mantle of uneasiness cloaked these lunches. This arose from the dilemma of whether it was appropriate, or even allowed, to order alcoholic beverages. Everyone remembers it as an awkward time, which is exactly what it was. To tell the truth the awkwardness and uneasiness at these lunches hung in the air like a San Francisco fog. It was quite serious really and threatened to destroy an otherwise amiable institution until one day the boss arrived unannounced and ordered a Manhattan. There was an almost audible sigh of relief when he sat down and joined us, but we all watched carefully to see if he'd order another, which he didn't. After that some ground rules were established: one or two glasses of wine or beer was acceptable, or one cocktail, provided it was something simple and elegant like a martini. Scotch was frowned on in general because everyone agreed it was a drink that should be reserved for evenings and drinking alone at a bar when you were depressed about something. Of course all this went out the window on Fridays (casual dress!) when anything was permissible and most of us left early anyway.

One of the unwritten, but well-adhered to, rules of the office is that we don't discuss politics or religion. One of the most distasteful episodes our office ever experienced came as a result of a political discussion, which to be accurate should really be referred to as an argument, or to be more accurate still, a brawl. This came about during the time that Jimmy Carter sent troops into Mozambique with the intention of assassinating several cabinet members of that government and a helicopter crashed and the whole operation turned into a big mess. That would have been all right except that there was one person in our office who was from Jimmy Carter's hometown and loved him like a father. It was no surprise then that when someone referred to Mr. Carter as "an ignorant peanut farmer" this other employee went, as the saying goes, "postal." It started out with some yelling and then some things were thrown and it wasn't long before there was some genuine Greco-Roman wrestling going on. When it was finally over, a chair had been broken, an office partition had been knocked down and the thermostat was left dangling from the wall by two thin red wires. For the next three days the state-of-the-art climate control system kept the place at a balmy eighty-five degrees and ninety-two percent humidity so that we all had to resort to wearing shorts and sandals. Even today the faint smell of coconut oil lingers on some of the upholstered chairs in the conference room.

One of the few rules at the office that is hard and fast and is actually printed in the Office Employee Policy Manual is that there is to be no intra-office dating. This is one of those rules that is ignored completely and is at least partially contradicted by the fact that there are condom machines in both bathrooms. At last count there was not a single office employee that hadn't been out on a date with another and this statistic includes the boss. Years ago there was one office employee whose family had roots in Italy and considered himself a bit of a Casanova. Over the course of six months he dated all but two women in the office and he probably would have dated them too if they hadn't been dating each other. Surprisingly this didn't create the turmoil you might expect. It turns out that he was an extremely nice guy who possessed a genuine love of women. In fact, he loved them to the point of worshiping them, which was flattering at first, but in the end (like after fifteen minutes) became extremely annoying. Needless to say, he's no longer with the company, although everyone remembers him fondly.

One of the few times when flex time becomes nonflexible is on Tuesday mornings at nine o'clock when there is a mandatory office staff meeting. This is the time when we all bring our cups of coffee into the conference room and complain about how much we have on our plates and how the bureaucracy of the corporate office is driving us to an early grave. Despite the complaining everyone is usually in a generally amiable mood because it isn't Monday, after all, and the conference room has no fewer than twelve sprinkler heads embedded in the ceiling, which is probably twice what code demands. Invariably at these meetings we all make excuses for why we haven't completed last week's action items then someone inevitably suggests that we attempt to "think outside the box." Then a colorful flow chart is presented and someone jots some things down on the white board and everyone is assigned new action items and after an hour we all go back to our cubicles, refilling our coffee on the way. Also, there are usually bagels with cream cheese that are quite good, even if they are always tainted with the faint taste of coconut oil.

Yes, when it comes to employment it's hard to beat the office. It's worth working here for the office parties alone. The best party is undoubtedly the annual Christmas party when we rent out the Elk Lodge and hire a local band. One year we had a punk band called The Lawn Ornaments. Everyone enjoys these parties enormously because we've just received our yearly bonuses and because the boss always springs for an open bar, which we are all able to make prodigious use of because we've all booked rooms across the street at the Super 8. There's a lot of dancing at these parties and not a little groping. Sometimes it's just fun to see if someone is trying to lead or is just holding the other person up. Anyway, after the party we've got an entire week off and by the time we come back to work everyone's essentially forgotten all the dumb things they said and whether the room they slept in at the Super 8 was actually the one they booked. All in all, it's a good time.

But really the best thing about the office is the sense that we're not just employees, not just gears in the corporate cog, but that we're members of a family—an incestuous family, granted, but family nonetheless. There's a lot to be said for this. Everyone agrees that essentially we're kin, that we're here for each other, that when push comes to shove we'd sacrifice our personal needs for the needs of others. Just the other day Ed's car broke down and he had no way to get home after work. When he asked Sally, someone in accounting, if she could give him a lift home, she said, *Screw you.* But then of course she drove him home. Just like a real sister would.

THE INEPT

FOR WEEKS AFTER I was laid off all I did was walk around the house in my underwear drinking coffee and beer and making up grandiose stories in my head about how I was this famous person or that. I kept the television on; the soap operas bored me to tears but I began to develop a fascination with celebrity couples. When I tried to do a little cleaning I'd get halfway through a job and move onto another. My wife was always coming home and having to put away the Windex and Lysol containers that I'd left lying around. One day I decided to make a bonsai tree out of some of our rosebushes, but I made a mess of it and had to uproot them and throw them in the trash. That's when I knew it was really getting bad, when I started doing things like that.

There was a time when I was working one day a week for a local newspaper and Jane, my wife, wasn't working at all. Strangely, those were the happiest days of our marriage. We drove out to the beach almost every day and lay around in the sun. We talked about how sweet our lives would be when she had a full-time teaching position at the university and I was a famous novelist. We were so happy to have all that ahead of us, and just to talk about it. It didn't even matter to us then if any of it actually ever happened. What did happen we had never imagined. I got laid off and Jane got a job with a local movie company as the assistant to the producer. Then for weeks all I could do was wander around the house aimlessly and couldn't keep my attention on one thing for more than a minute. One day I went to the store and bought a set of lawn darts. But then I threw one too far and almost killed the neighbor's dog so I threw them in the trash with the rosebushes. Half the time I spent worrying about whether Jane was having sex with the producer. Every time I brought it up Jane would make love to me fiercely and swear that she was bound to me forever and nothing could change that, but still I worried. I was going downhill fast. I was going crazy. Then, surprise, surprise, Jane's sister died and her retarded son came to live with us. That's what changed everything.

I don't know what today's definition of retarded is, but I saw right off that this kid had more going for him than I did. The very first day he made me get dressed and take him to the farmer's market. He bought sun-dried tomatoes, mushrooms, onions, jalapeños, and then he made us an omelet that melted in my mouth. The next day he wanted to go kayaking, so we rented some boats, bought a twelve-pack of beer and floated the river all day. The kid was always clapping his hands. He applauded everything from a sparrow hopping around in the grass to a drunk stumbling down the street. One time I told him how long it had been since I'd had a job and he clapped like crazy. Man, did that make me feel good. I even told him that I thought Jane was having an affair with her producer and he clapped like a maniac then. Pretty soon he had me doing it. When the clutch went out in my truck we both got out and applauded. We laughed so hard we fell down right in the road. The kid really showed me how to look on the bright side of things.

One day we loaded up the car and went to the state park for the day to have a picnic. There was a large motorcycle gang nearby, smoking grass and playing Frisbee. They had a small puppy that caught the kid's attention. He watched and watched and begged me to let him go play with it, but I didn't think it was a good idea, so I didn't let him. We grilled our steaks and ate potato salad until we couldn't stand up. Then I drifted off to sleep for a while under a tree.

When I woke up the kid was down by the river with

two of the women from the motorcycle gang. They were kneeling at the edge of the water like I'd seen kids do on science field trips. I walked over and saw what they were looking at. The puppy was lying on the shore with its tongue out. I could see right away that it had drowned. The kid was stroking the puppy's wet head with the back of his hand. Both the women were crying. I stood several feet away and watched. I began crying myself. The puppy looked so pitiful and I couldn't help thinking about how full of life it had been just hours before. The women didn't interrupt the kid. They just let him stroke the puppy's head like a priest. I think we all thought the kid could bring that little dog back to life. After a while, two or three others from the gang joined us and stood silently watching the kid. I felt like I was at a family funeral. One of the men even put his hand on my shoulder. Then the kid did something miraculous. He stood up and spread his arms apart like he'd been nailed to a cross. Suddenly we were all engulfed in silence and nothingness. Even the river was quiet. Then he brought his hands together and started clapping. The cracking of his hands together filled our ears like exploding fireworks. One by one we all joined him. Before long the woods were full of our applause. By that time a crowd of the sorrowful and the inept had gathered.

LEIF PETERSON is the author of the novel *Catherine Wheels*. His stories regularly appear in magazines and journals nationwide. He lives with his wife and children in Northwest Montana where he writes and raises pheasants.

Made in the USA